WE FORGET NOTHING

FBI TASK FORCE S.W.O.R.D.
BOOK 2

D.D. BLACK

DARKNESS AND LIGHT PUBLISHING

PART 1

THE HELL INSIDE US

"There is no greater sorrow than to recall
our times of joy in wretchedness."
- Dante

"We become what we love and who we love
shapes what we become."
- St. Clare of Assisi

"Heaven has no rage like love to hatred turned,
Nor hell a fury like a woman scorned."
- William Congreve

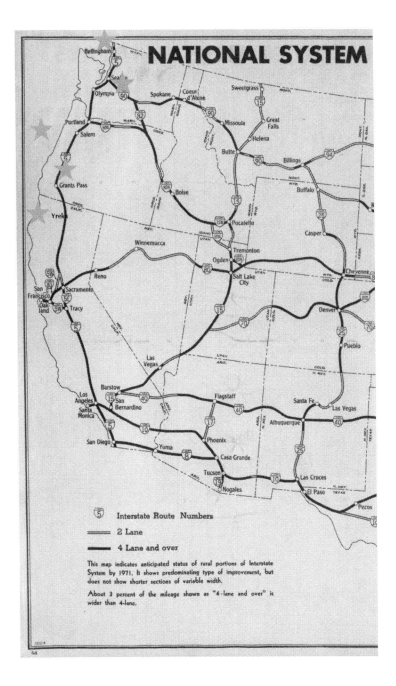

NATIONAL SYSTEM

⑤ Interstate Route Numbers

══════ 2 Lane

▬▬▬▬ 4 Lane and over

This map indicates anticipated status of rural portions of Interstate System by 1971. It shows predominating type of improvement, but does not show shorter sections of variable width.

About 3 percent of the mileage shown as "4-lane and over" is wider than 4-lane.

CHAPTER ONE

Evergreen Memory Care

Seattle, Washington

FOR THE FIRST FEW MONTHS, Lydia didn't notice anything strange about Augustus Cunningham. Maybe he made an odd comment here or there, sure. But odd comments were a dime a dozen at *Evergreen Memory Care*. On the morning everything changed, she was serving breakfast as usual.

Breakfast was one of the toughest shifts. The state surveyors were big on facilities like Evergreen offering choices to their patients. It was part of the requirement for individualized care plans and patient dignity and all that.

At every meal there were choices, but at breakfast the choices were far more complex. Cereal, or bacon and eggs? What kind of bread for your toast? What kind of jam? Tea or coffee with your juice? And the cereal, coffee, tea, and juice options were endless.

Add in the fact that she was dealing with memory care patients, and taking an order could take forever. Of course, Lydia knew better than to call them "patients" in front of management. *At Evergreen Memory Care, we treat residents like they're our guests.* At least that's what it said on the brochure.

"Good morning, Sister Ella," Lydia said, "would you like eggs or oatmeal for breakfast this morning?"

"What is it my child?" Sister Ella asked. She was eighty-odd years old and permanently bent forward by osteoporosis. Sister Ella did everything together with the two women who shared her table, Sister Ruth and Sister Veronica.

It was possible to get by without knowing about a resident's past, but Lydia was curious by nature and dipped into the charts when she had a spare moment. She also asked a lot of questions. She'd seen pictures of these three in their younger years standing in front of large hydraulic ferry ramps wearing orange safety vests over the same simple brown habits they wore to this day. The nuns were from the Franciscan order that had run the ferry terminal on Shaw Island since the 1970s. Now they were too old to work and had no novice nuns to replace them—or take care of them.

Lydia examined Ella's ears; she wasn't wearing her hearing aids. The morning medpass had been heavy, and somewhere in the revolving door of nursing staff, Ella's hearing aids had been forgotten. Again.

Lydia crouched down, placed her hand on Sister Ella's arm, then spoke clearly, trying not to sound exasperated or impatient. "Would you like eggs or oatmeal this morning?"

Sister Ella patted Lydia on the hand and smiled, then turned to Sister Ruth, who sat to her right. "I deeply apologize for being late for the ferry. Please forgive me. Somehow I've missed morning prayers *and* breakfast."

The plates landed on the table with a *clunk, clunk, clunk.*

Lydia's coworker Debbie had dollupped oatmeal topped

with slivered almonds into three small bowls that each sat on a plate next to an underripe banana. "You know this is all they ever end up eating," Debbie snapped. "We have another sixty-some people to feed this morning, right? Put a fire under it."

Debbie took a full glass of milk from the table where residents who were unable to feed themselves sat waiting for a caregiver. She poured it over the three oatmeals.

Lydia peeled and sliced the banana for Sister Veronica. She was the most confused of the three and Lydia didn't want to find her choking if she tried to eat the whole banana, peel and all, as she had last week.

Lydia left the dining room to serve Geraldine, who preferred to take breakfast in her room. Every morning the same sweet, nearly toothless smile would greet her.

"Ah Lydia," Geraldine sang as she walked in, "*she was the most glorious creature under the sun...*" Geraldine was one of the few residents who remembered Lydia's name, and she loved to sing a song about it.

Glancing past Geraldine at her own reflection in the armoire mirror, Lydia admired her bright red, shoulder length hair, which she'd dyed the night before. Not that anyone here would notice.

"Well, honey, there's a problem," Geraldine said, "I can't seem to find my purse. Now, I don't want you to think I'm trying to cadge a free meal, if you'll just give me a chance to look around a bit—"

"Don't you worry about it, Geraldine, breakfast is on the house." Lydia spoke in her buddy-buddy tone. Letting residents think they were getting a free meal was a small pleasure, and those were highly valued commodities in a place like this.

"Really?"

"Yep. No charge, sweetie. Don't you worry about it."

From experience, Lydia knew that there was a fifty-fifty chance Geraldine would remember that she didn't have to pay for lunch, but by tomorrow's breakfast she would once again be looking for her purse. Memory worked in mysterious ways.

Lydia took Geraldine's order, brought her breakfast, then returned to the dining area.

And so it went: Francine sat rocking back and forth silently, eventually eating whatever was put in front of her. Mary angrily demanded to know what all these people were doing in her grandmother's house. Lloyd, enjoying his breakfast, confided in Lydia, as he did every day, that this would be his last morning here as his son would be taking him home this afternoon.

He'd told Lydia that nearly every day for two years, undeterred by the death of his son eight months ago. Lydia would go along with his delusion, smile, and wish him a pleasant trip just as she always had. If her little lie offered him a moment of joy, it was worth any time she would spend in purgatory cleansing herself of it.

Augustus—who preferred to be called Gus—had been at Evergreen for nearly a year and preferred to sit at a table alone by the window.

Always alone.

Always by the window.

He didn't look up when she slid the breakfast tray in front of him. Dry toast, an empty bowl, a glass of milk. He placed the toast in the bowl and poured the milk over it, then began mashing.

Lydia hadn't heard of milktoast before Gus came to live at Evergreen. And, despite his memory issues, remembering to demand milktoast every morning was not something he ever forgot.

He took one bite, then looked up at Lydia.

She watched as his expression changed to a look she read as frustration.

"Everything okay, Gus?" Lydia asked, crouching next to him to inspect his meal. "Is something wrong with your breakfast? We have raisin toast today. If you would like that instead, I will get you some."

His stare lingered and he flared his nostrils. His upper lip lifted briefly in a snarl, revealing several yellowed teeth. Soggy white toast clumps filled in gaps where his gums had receded. His look turned ominous as his eyes darkened and his pupils grew large and glossy.

Lydia's instincts to bolt kicked in a moment too late.

As she tried to stand, he grabbed her by the hair, then pulled her closer, his grip firmer than she'd thought him capable of.

"What a *nuisance!*" he hissed viciously, the deep wrinkles on his weathered face growing stiff.

Despite the pain in her scalp, her ears perked at the voice. The phrase. Both were familiar, but from where?

She grabbed Gus's hand, then pried gently, trying not to hurt him, slowly kneeling next to him to prevent him from ripping the hair from her scalp. "Gus, everything's okay. It's Lydia. You're here at Evergreen Memory Care in Seattle. Everything's okay. Now eat your milktoast before it gets too..." She trailed off. She was going to say *cold*, then she was going to say *mushy*. But the breakfast he ate was already cold and always mushy. "Please eat your milktoast, Gus." She pushed the bowl towards him. "Look at your milktoast here, just the way you like it," she continued, keeping her voice calm and sweet.

Finally, Gus turned his attention to the bowl and loosened his grip on her hair. Lydia used his moment of distraction to rip her hair from his hand, then rapidly stumbled backwards in an awkward crabwalk to get away.

Lydia had been working at Evergreen Memory Care in Seattle for five years, which made her a seasoned veteran by staffing standards. Six months was average turnover for anything below management, and management wasn't a great deal better.

She'd seen a lot and heard even more. She'd dealt with plenty of combative patients, but she'd never seen anything like the look Gus gave her today. His sharp gaze felt like it could have pierced her skull. It had certainly pierced her soul.

And the way he'd said *nuisance* was eerily familiar.

That night, alone in her little studio apartment, Lydia rubbed at her sore scalp and scanned her laptop screen. She spent many hours a week in the online forums, chat rooms, and Facebook groups dedicated to true crime mysteries.

In fact, she was a self-professed true crime junkie. She was obsessed with cold cases, the search for justice, and the enigmatic killers who'd never been caught. The cases were like little puzzles in her head and she loved moving the pieces around. She'd never thought she would actually *solve* anything, but today everything on the screen was lining up.

The Interstate Reaper had killed five women between 1979 and 1989, up and down Interstate 5, from Northern California all the way up to close to the Canadian border in Bellingham, Washington.

And they were all redheads.

Gus Cunningham was ninety years old, with a gaunt frame and thin white hair. He didn't look like he could do much more than pull a woman's hair now. His age was spot on, and what she knew of his background lined up as well. Gus had worked as a manager for a chain of diners that had expanded from Northern California up I-5 in the seventies and eighties.

But it wasn't just that.

One of the only pieces of evidence in the case, which was one of the coldest in the history of serial killers, was a recording of a man in a little campground in Yreka, California. It had been caught by accident by a local film crew shooting a promotional video for California's tourism bureau. The film crew had discovered the audio a week later, and only thought anything of it because a woman's strangled corpse had been found only a hundred yards from where they'd been filming.

Now, Lydia clicked over to the page where all the evidence in the case was pored over by true crime fanatics like her. Pictures of the victims, timelines of the killings, a list of suspects, all of whom had been dismissed decades earlier for their solid alibis or lack of evidence.

She found the audio and clicked *Play*.

It was scratchy and far away, but had been amplified with modern technology. The voice sounded younger, but it definitely could have been Gus Cunningham.

"What a *nuisance!*"

"So, Mr. Cunningham," she began the next morning as she slid his toast and milk in front of him, careful to keep out of arm's reach, "I hear you used to be Regional Manager for the Sunny Skillet Diner chain. That must have been interesting work, huh?"

She hoped he was in one of his lucid states, but it appeared that he wasn't. He set the toast in the bowl and poured the milk over it, then began his mashing ritual.

"That job must have taken you from California all the

way through Oregon and into Washington," she continued, making sure to keep a solid object like a chair between them. Although he didn't appear as sinister as he had the day before, she didn't want to take any chances. "Quite a lot of time on Interstate 5. A lot of miles, right?"

He said nothing.

"Mr. Cunningham, you know I've eaten at those diners my whole life. Best chicken and waffles I've ever had." He took a pitiful spoonful into his mouth and looked out the window as he processed the mush before swallowing.

"Mr. Cunningham, don't tell me you've forgotten about Sunny Skillet Diner. You worked there for over thirty years." She was trying to sound friendly. "Have you forgotten? Why, there's likely no one alive who's more responsible for my appreciation of southern comfort food. I always wanted red hair just like the little girl in the commercial. Mine's from a bottle, dyed you know. Do you like it?"

Gus didn't respond.

Lydia thought about how memories of people suffering with dementia can sometimes be triggered by songs from their past. "You remember that commercial, don't you? With the little girl? *Nothing gives you that feeling of a nice sunny day like a Sunny Skillet Diner meal.* You could never forget that song."

At this, Gus threw his spoon into the bowl. Milk and soggy mash slopped over the side and the bowl rattled to a stop. He looked up, twisting his neck. His eyes moved from her face to her hair slowly, then back to her face until his eyes were locked on hers.

"Forget?" He paused, his yellow teeth breaking into a wicked smile. "We forget nothing, you little *nuisance*."

CHAPTER TWO

"EITHER OF YOU know anything about salmon fishing?" Claire asked.

She stood in the lobby of the FBI headquarters in Seattle, waiting in line at the little coffee stand for her first caffeinated beverage of the morning. To her left stood Jack Russo, and to her right, Fitz Pembroke, III. They had been arguing back and forth about who would handle the rest of the paperwork from the case of the Luminist Killer, whom they had brought down about six weeks earlier.

"I can't say that I do," Fitz said, "but I know that late April is not the ideal salmon fishing season in this region." Ranger, their Golden Retriever, left Fitz's side and nudged his ear against Claire's leg, then sat and looked up at her.

Out of the four of them, Ranger looked like the one most likely to know something about fish. The green nylon tactical vest he wore made him look like he could be carrying fishing tackle. Put a salmon in his mouth and he'd make the front page of *Northwest Sportsman*.

"Fitz, how do you know that random detail?" Claire asked. She reached down and scratched Ranger behind the ears. "I mean, I asked both of you, but I was really asking Jack."

Jack had grown up on a ranch and seemed like the kind of guy who'd also know how to fish. Fitz, on the other hand, was the type to be found at home with his face either in a book or a pint of lager.

"The salmon fishing season in Washington is one of a million pieces of fairly useless information I have at the ready." Fitz smiled. "Useless to me, that is, as I am not someone who has ever—or *will* ever—stand on the beach casting a line and waiting hopefully. But it might just be useful to a case, or to you. Isn't that why you brought me onto the team?"

Claire sighed.

Jack came up alongside Fitz and patted him on the shoulder. "Do all Brits like to hear themselves talk as much as you do?"

"Not at all," Fitz said. "My countrymen are known for being stoic and emotionally withdrawn. In a good way. Please don't take my personal failings as representative of the great United Kingdom."

"Bob's my uncle," Jack said.

"Meh," Fitz responded.

They reached the front of the line and Claire ordered her cappuccino. Jack ordered a black coffee, and Fitz, after considering his options for well over a minute—even though he'd had plenty of time to decide what to order while standing in line—ordered a can of Coke.

Claire wasn't surprised, but Jack's eyes widened. "I can't believe you're drinking *Coke* at eight in the morning."

"Back in the UK," Fitz replied, "it's well after noon."

Claire frowned. "You haven't lived in the UK in ten years."

"You can take the bloke out of England—" Fitz began.

"Oh right, Fitzie," Claire interrupted. "I forgot you were banned from the country permanently."

"Banned? Not at all," Fitz said. "Highly discouraged from returning by multiple government agencies? Possibly."

"Wait, really?" Jack asked. "I mean I knew you screwed up over there, but—"

"Not really," Claire said. "Just a running joke we share."

"Yeah," Fitz said, clearing his throat dramatically. "A joke. To be sure."

Claire saw Jack's confusion. "Fitz's family is placed throughout the top echelon of both business and politics over there. He jokes that if he ever tries to return home they'll stop him at the airport and send him on the first flight out of England to a lovely town by the name of *Anywhere Else*, to avoid embarrassment."

"Not just embarrassment," Fitz said. "Utter scandal."

The barista handed Fitz the can of Coke. Standing out against Fitz's brown corduroy sports coat, the same one he always wore, the bright red can struck Claire's senses in the otherwise drab lobby setting.

She rubbed at her ribs, which had healed well from her recent fight, but still stung from time to time. She knew enough to know that the pain was related to the emotional trauma of her previous case, but that didn't make it go away.

For the last six weeks, her task force had been looking into various cold cases from the FBI's past. Although she had been ready to take on any new cases that arose, she knew that solving a major case from the past would bring her team the departmental recognition she wanted. And she didn't want it for selfish reasons. Ever since the formation of Task Force S.W.O.R.D., she'd been battling to get the money and resources she needed to do it right.

"Why'd you want to know about fishing?" Jack asked as they ambled across the lobby.

"Benny," Claire said, her heart tugging a little. "We play this fish game online. And since he's on his computer so much, I want to get him outside for the real thing. My ex-husband always said he'd take him fishing, but well..."

"One of his *many* failings," Fitz said, nodding in understanding.

"Let's not badmouth my husband," Claire said.

As frustrated as she'd been—and still was—with Brian, she'd told herself she'd never speak badly about him outside of her closest friends or her therapist. For better or worse, he was the father of her children and deserved a modicum of respect, despite his failings.

"*Ex*-husband, I thought," Fitz added.

Claire shot him a narrow-eyed look.

Obviously taking the hint, Fitz zipped his lips.

"Anyway," she continued, "I told Benny I'd take him fishing or would find someone who was an expert. You two are the closest thing he has to uncles, God help us all."

Fitz laughed.

"I can take him," Jack said. "Lake fishing is really my speciality. But I've been meaning to go out there and toss a line for some salmon one of these days."

"Thanks," Claire said. "I know he'll—"

She stopped mid sentence when she heard a woman speaking loudly by the entry gate.

"I need to speak with someone *now!*" the woman was saying, her voice oscillating between agitated and frantic.

Claire studied her from across the lobby. She had bright red hair, obviously dyed, and appeared to be in her mid forties. She was short, with a medium build and a dark tattoo on her wrist that Claire couldn't make out from across the lobby. Judging by her brightly-colored, polka-dotted scrubs, she was a nurse or CNA.

"Wait here," Claire said to Fitz and Jack, walking over to her.

The woman was growing more and more agitated each time the security guard refused to let her through, but she didn't strike Claire as a threat. More than anything, she appeared afraid. But people who were in danger usually called the police, or went to their local precinct.

"Really!" the woman implored, now nearing tears. "I need to speak with someone in the FBI. It's important."

Claire stopped a few paces away.

"Ma'am," the security guard said, his voice a long, uninterested drawl, "if you don't have an appointment, you can't just come in demanding to be heard. That's not how this works."

"The Interstate Reaper," the woman said. "I found him."

Claire cocked her head slightly. She knew about the case. Everyone in the FBI knew about it. Damn near everyone in America had at least heard of it.

Apparently the security guard wasn't one of them. "Now, I don't know who that is or who you *think* that is, but it won't help you get in here. You need to call ahead and make an appointment with one of our agents."

"The Interstate Reaper..." the woman said again.

"You understand, right?" the security guard said, waving her away. "If we let everyone just show up at our doorstep, nothing would get done."

There were tears forming in the woman's eyes and her cheeks had reddened. "The Interstate Reaper is living fifteen minutes from here. I'm *literally* his nurse."

Claire stepped forward and put her hand on the security guard's raised desk. "What's your name?" she asked the woman.

The security guard threw up his hands in a way Claire felt was his best attempt at subtlety, then walked a few steps away from the desk muttering something about sticking to protocol.

"Lydia," the woman said, wiping away tears. "Lydia Ramirez."

Claire studied her. What had looked like polka dots from further away were actually little strawberries, some of them with a bite taken out. "I take it from your scrubs that you don't work in law enforcement?"

She shook her head. "Memory care facility. I'm a CNA. Certified Nursing Assistant."

Claire nodded. "And you have some information on the Interstate Reaper case?"

"Information? No, I have the killer. I mean I work with him, or *for* him, or... I mean every morning I give him milk-toast. Well, when I'm working, actually, but I—"

"Please," Claire said, "let's just slow down."

The tears were rolling down Lydia's cheeks now and she was taking quick, short breaths.

Claire knew about the online culture of amateur sleuths, and knew well that they were almost always delusional or misinformed. The FBI tip line got calls every week from random people who believed they'd solved this crime or that one. Usually they turned out to be from random guys living in their mom's basement or paranoid women with twenty-seven cats and too much free time.

But something about Lydia Ramirez struck her as genuine.

Claire smiled at the security guard. "Ahmed," she said, "it's all right. Get Lydia's ID and whatnot, and send her down to the Boiler Room. I think she might have something we need to hear."

CHAPTER THREE

TWENTY MINUTES LATER, Lydia sat in Claire's usual spot in the Boiler Room.

Fitz, Jack, and Kiko took one side of the table. Violet sat in her usual spot in the corner, facing her three computer screens instead of the room. And Ranger lay in his usual spot in the middle of the room next to the fancy dog bed Fitz had bought for him that he never used. Fitz had decided to move the bed to the center of the room thinking that placement had been the problem. It wasn't. As always, Ranger had inspected the newcomer upon entry and given her his blessing to enter before returning to his nap.

Claire leaned against the wall. "Ms. Ramirez, please start from the beginning."

To Claire's surprise, Lydia had completely regained her composure, shaken off her tears, and now seemed poised to interview Claire, instead of vice versa. "How much do you know about the Interstate Reaper?" Lydia asked.

Slightly embarrassed, Claire said, "I know the basics, but I haven't read any of the files."

"It's actually one of the most exciting cold cases we have," Lydia said. "The online community is just nuts for it. It wasn't one of my specialties until recently."

Claire had noticed Jack leaning forward, and now he could no longer contain himself. "Wait, wait, *wait.* 'One of the most exciting cold cases we have?' You sound like you think you're the lead investigator or something. I thought you were a CNA at a memory care facility."

"I *am* a CNA," Lydia said. "But I'm a true crime fighter, too. Well, not a *fighter*, more of a fan. I mean, less of a fan, just an interested person or whatever. It's a hobby, you know?"

With a glance, Claire told Jack to back off, but she shared his frustration. Sometime in the last ten or fifteen years, the culture had taken a strange turn. True crime shows, books, and podcasts had flourished like never before, and it seemed as though hundreds of online communities had sprung up around dissecting evidence from old cases. It wasn't that she didn't think it was possible for an amateur to figure out something of value, but many of the online communities descended into conspiracy theories—often about the FBI or police fabricating or covering up evidence—as well as oddball theories and plain nonsense.

Lydia was about to continue, but Claire held up a hand. "Violet, can you pull up a summary?"

"Already on it," Violet said from the corner without turning around.

Claire had gotten used to her baggy sweatshirts and jet black hair sometimes being the only thing she saw of Violet all day.

The large monitor on the wall flickered to life and Claire saw a body lying on a pebbly beach, mostly covered. A single foot stuck out at the bottom of a white sheet, pale against the blue and gray stones. The photo was obviously from the seventies, based on its slightly muted color palette.

"In 1979," Violet began, "a 59-year-old woman was abducted from a local campground near Lake Whatcom. Sandra Ireland was her name and she was said to enjoy long solitary walks and—I swear I'm not making this up, it's in the file—*disco* music. Her remains were discovered by hikers in some brambles about five yards from the water on this beach in Bellingham, Washington.

"The following year," Violet continued, as Claire watched images of the deceased women appear on the screen, "on May 22, 1980, just outside of Grants Pass, Oregon, a 56-year-old transient woman who occasionally stayed in local parks was abducted from a bus stop. A jogger later found her body in a secluded part of the park. Tom Pearce Park on the Rogue River. Her name was Francis Graber.

"Spring of 1983 Portland, Oregon. On April 3, a 61-year-old woman named Pamela Krane, struggling with addiction, often seen near SE 82nd Avenue, was abducted. Her body was later discovered in a wooded area near Crystal Springs Lake not far from Reed College, right in the city. That was a bit of an aberration.

"In 1986, a 60-year-old woman known for her frequent walks in Discovery Park, Seattle, was the next victim. Her name was Caroline Smith and she was abducted from the park and her body was found hidden in dense foliage next to a little area of wetlands called Utah Wetlands on June 10."

The photo changed again and Claire had already picked up a pattern. All of them were redheads—like Lydia herself —and all had been found in parks or other natural areas.

For a moment she wondered whether it was appropriate to view the photos with Lydia in the room, but they were all in the public record and no doubt Lydia had seen them already.

"Finally," Violet said, "the most recent case occurred in 1989 in Yreka, California. A 58-year-old woman named Susan Swanson was last seen at a remote campground near the Klamath River on August 5. Her body was found the next day." Violet paused and, though her typical tone of voice was fairly matter-of-fact, now Claire could hear the frustration building. "All were strangled with a belt. Fiber evidence points to the *same* belt. No connections between the victims, other than the red hair. No evidence of sexual assault in any of the cases. There were a handful of suspects, and obviously both local police and the FBI looked into the fact that all five women were found near Interstate 5. But then the killings stopped and, after 1989, the case went colder than last year's leftover dumplings, lost to the back of a freezer."

"Maybe we should get dumplings for lunch," Fitz said, but no one bothered to respond. This was no joking matter.

"When I dyed my hair red," Lydia said, "the patient got aggressive with me. Scared me. Everyone knows he has some vendetta against redheads. He—"

"What else?" Jack asked, turning his attention from the screen to Lydia. "What do you think you know?"

"Let her finish, you numbskull," Fitz said.

"There *is* something else," Lydia said, "something that tied it all together. One of the key pieces of evidence, one of the *only* pieces of evidence, is that there was an audio recording that happened only minutes before one of the murders. The evidence wasn't discovered until well after, but they have the killer's voice on tape." She made her voice a deep hiss. "'You little *nuisance.*'"

Claire had heard the recording.

"When I brought up elements of his past," Lydia said, "that is *exactly* what Augustus Cunningham said to me."

She leaned back and folded her arms, glaring at Jack as though challenging him to challenge her.

"There could be a lot of reasons for that," Claire said carefully. "That was one detail I'd heard about, and I know it was widely reported in the press. But it's enough to check it out." She turned and addressed the back of Violet's head. "Violet, can we match a voice from audio that old with audio from a man today? That is, if this *is* the same person, if we record the 90-year-old Augustus Cunningham's voice today, can we conclusively match it with that tiny snippet from 1989?"

Violet had already located the audio in question and she played it through the Boiler Room sound system. "What a *nuisance*."

The clip was scratchy and faint, but clear enough to make out the words.

She played it again. "What a *nuisance*."

The voice chilled Claire. What might otherwise have been a benign comment turned evil filtered through an icey, rageful voice.

And again. "What a *nuisance*."

"That's enough," Claire said.

"I will admit," Lydia said, "he doesn't sound much like that anymore."

"The technology on this is difficult," Violet said. "Could we potentially get a match? Yes. And if we decide to take this any further, it's worth a shot."

"I sense a *but* coming," Claire said.

"Would it be definitive in any way or hold up in court?" Violet asked. "No."

"And there's no DNA evidence, correct?" Jack asked.

"Not yet," Fitz said. "But technology has come a long

way since this case went cold. Assuming some of the clothes from the victims are still in storage, we could have the lab try again, matching against current DNA from Cunningham."

Claire was growing uncomfortable. Discussing publicly known details was one thing, but they shouldn't have been discussing this in front of someone outside the team.

"Let's get back to your experience, Ms. Ramirez. Can you tell us a little bit about your job, and your day-to-day interactions with your patients?"

CHAPTER FOUR

THE INTERVIEW CONTINUED for another twenty minutes, but Lydia provided little actual evidence. Most of what she gave them had to do with Gus Cunningham's past and his daily habits inside Evergreen Memory Care. Before today Claire had never heard of milktoast. She figured it had to do with aging—maybe he had a delicate system or needed to eat only soft foods, but she found it sad that the regional manager of the Sunny Skillet Diner chain would be found subsisting on such an uninspired meal.

In the end, Claire was interested enough to follow up, but unconvinced that they'd stumbled on the Interstate Reaper. She had Kiko walk Lydia out to the lobby, then stepped out into the hallway to find a second liquid caffeine injection. She needed to pad her emotions with legal stimulants before her meeting with Gerald Hightower.

Halfway to the breakroom, Claire froze.

Leaning on the wall at the end of the hallway and chatting with a secretary was Jonathan Rivera, the SAC of the Administrative Division in Seattle. Jon Rivera or *J-River*, as he claimed he'd been called back when he played football.

The thorn in her side. The pebble in her shoe. The pain in her kiester.

She wasn't afraid of him. Not exactly, anyway. But he was the guy who'd ruined more of her days than she could count over the past six weeks. After taking on the assignment of managing the new Special Washington-Oregon Regional Detachment—FBI Task Force S.W.O.R.D.—Claire had been advocating for significant quality-of-life improvements within the office. A high-end coffee maker, a second vehicle, a new desk, and ergonomic chairs for the team. Rivera had blocked them all, arguing that the requests, while not unreasonable, had to be weighed against budget constraints and the needs of other divisions.

When she'd proposed transforming the S.W.O.R.D. meeting room into a state-of-the-art facility, equipped with the latest communication and presentation technologies, Rivera had pushed back, citing the substantial costs and logistical complications and pointing out that similar resources were available elsewhere in the building.

When she'd argued that having dedicated vehicles for S.W.O.R.D. would enhance their efficiency and response times, Rivera told her that the existing vehicle pool system was "designed to maximize resource utilization across all units," and that "exclusive allocation could set a difficult precedent."

For their investigations, Claire had requested cutting-edge software and technology tools that weren't standard issue within the FBI. Violet had assured her they'd make a difference. SAC Rivera had questioned the cost-benefit ratio of these tools, suggesting the use of alternatives already licensed to the FBI and emphasizing adherence to established procurement protocols.

In short, in the brief time S.W.O.R.D. had been in existence, Rivera had been its biggest opponent. The guy had even had the audacity to try to get Ranger kicked out of the building, citing potential increased medical expenses related to potential dog allergies.

Making her way down the hall, Claire met Rivera's eyes and he moved away from his discussion to face her. The secretary ambled off down the hall, sensing trouble. Everyone in the building knew that Claire and Rivera couldn't stand each other.

Claire made her voice light and positive, the catch-more-flies-with-honey approach. "Any progress on getting us that car?"

Rivera folded his arms. "No," he said casually.

At fifty, he carried the weight of his extensive experience in the FBI with a sort of quiet intensity. He had a compact, sturdy build, like a barrel reinforced with steel, and a face that never seemed to change its expression, as though the barrel had been topped with a perfectly round stone.

Claire regretted not getting total control of her budget when she agreed to lead the unit. It was great to have a good team of people, but without equipment, vehicles, and actual funding, it was difficult to get anything done.

"As you know," Rivera said, his voice deep, "terrorism remains our highest priority given the situation at the ports. I didn't approve of this unit to begin with and—"

"Thankfully," Claire interrupted, "it wasn't your role to approve it."

Rivera frowned. "I guess it wasn't. But no, we have *not* approved your new car."

Claire folded her arms. "I'll be talking with Hightower."

"Run to daddy all you like, but I think you know which of us is in charge of the purse strings."

Claire frowned. "What's your problem? You *do* know we're on the same team, right?"

He smirked. "I'm on the team of stopping terrorist attacks, not solving forty year old cold cases no one even remotely cares about anymore."

Claire was taken off guard.

"Oh yeah," Rivera said, a smirk coming through his voice despite his stone-faced stare, "it's going around the building that your *team* is talking to some kooky citizen investigator." He shook his head. "I hope you feel like you're making good use of your time, Agent Anderson. Time that, by the way, taxpayers foot the bill for. I assure you that I intend to continue to scrutinize and keep the budget trim."

Claire offered up a fake smile. "I'd expect nothing less."

"Do you know what *I* call the budget line item S.W.O.R.D.?"

"I don't, but judging by the smug look on your face, it's something as clever as *J-River*."

Rivera spoke through gritted teeth. "Superfluous Waste Organ Requiring Dismemberment." With that, he walked away.

As Claire headed towards the elevator, she let go of any aspiration she once had of adding wine to the snack budget.

CHAPTER FIVE

THAT AFTERNOON when Claire returned to the Boiler Room, it had transformed from a somewhat outdated basement office to something that looked more like the dorm room of a college student who had signed up for too many classes and had six assignments due the next day. Three large boxes sat in the corner, and stacks of papers and files took up half of the large desk in the center of the room. Even Ranger's dog bed was covered in papers.

Violet, who usually sat at her computer desk in the corner, was sitting at the table, looking flustered as she thumbed through a stack of yellowing paper.

She didn't even look up when Claire walked in. "How is it possible," Violet asked, "that we haven't digitized all of this stuff yet?"

"Because," Jack said, "the FBI likes to spend its time and money on things that are *actually* important."

"Rationing Rivera teach you that?" Claire asked. She could take guff from the SAC of the Administrative Division. Her own S.W.O.R.D. team members being dismissive would have to be nipped in the bud. "I need you to think long and hard about what you find important, Jack. Because if it isn't the work we are doing here today, I know a road you can hit."

"Plus," Fitz said, "this *is* bloody important." He looked at Claire, his eyes imploring. "You just got out of your meeting with Hightower, right?"

Claire nodded.

"And, let me guess," Fitz continued, now standing and walking over to the corner of the room where Ranger lay, snoring quietly. "You asked Hightower for more money and Hightower deferred to Rivera again? Hightower, having gotten you to sign on, is now stonewalling any budget requests you make. And it won't stop there, Claire. He will walk all over you and then the rest of us."

Fitz took a seat in one of the less sturdy metal chairs, his heavy frame slightly warping the front legs as he leaned forward to scratch Ranger behind the ears.

"And how does that relate to this case?" Claire asked.

"Sure," Fitz said, "this case might not be the most important crime in the world. It's old. Key players have moved on or—more than likely—met their maker." He stood slowly, but didn't topple over as Claire expected. He'd slowed down with his after-hours drinking, Claire knew, but he still wore the same brown sports coat he always wore and still didn't bathe nearly enough for her liking. "But it garners massive public interest, as do all serial killer cold cases. If we can get to the bottom of it, it would do wonders for the credibility of this outfit."

"Or," Jack said, his voice dripping with sarcasm, "we could waste weeks of our time and get nowhere on a case that poses no imminent threat to the public."

"I'm with Fitz on this," Kiko said. She had been fairly

quiet all day, so Claire was almost surprised to hear her voice. "I don't think that woman was acting. I think she was genuinely terrified, and probably for good reason. Sure, the evidence she provided was weak, but that doesn't mean it's wrong."

Claire glanced down at her watch. It was nearly 3:30, and she had to leave a little bit early today. Benny was taking the ferry by himself for the first time. He'd be arriving in downtown Seattle at 4:30. His thirteenth birthday was coming up, and he was becoming increasingly well known in various online forums for his YouTube channel, *Down with Gaming*. And recently he'd been invited to tour a video game company in Seattle. He had been more excited about this invitation than she'd seen him in years, and she'd agree to take off a little bit early to accompany him on the tour.

Claire pointed at the chair that Fitz had just vacated. "Please sit down," she said. He did, and Claire sat across from him. "Okay, I have fifteen minutes before I have to leave. Let's pretend as though this *is* our case." She turned to Jack. "Where would you start?"

Jack folded his arms and sighed. "I hope we are *only* going to give this fifteen minutes, but I'd start with the suspects. Good men and women worked on this case for years, and I'm sure there's a decent amount to gain from the sweat equity that's already been put in."

Violet stood and moved back over to her computers. "And the suspect list is one of the *only* things that actually has been digitized. There's no mention of Augustus Cunningham, unfortunately, as that would make our job a heck of a lot easier. But Jack is right. A lot of work has been done." She tapped away at one of her keyboards and the big monitor on the wall lit up. "First, we have Michael Trenton, now deceased. He was a long-haul trucker known for his routes along I-5, fitting the geographic profile of the murders. He was between the ages of fifty and sixty when the murders took place."

As she spoke, Violet tapped away, making a series of photos pop up on the screen.

Trenton was a burly man with a weathered face marked by deep lines and a graying beard. His eyes, a faded blue, appeared tired and only a few strands of hair were visible under the *Freeman's Beer* cap he wore in every photo.

"Trenton passed away from natural causes five years ago. Despite several interviews and searches, no physical evidence was ever linked to him, but his travel logs placed him near several of the crime scenes. Next," Violet continued, "we have Eric Kilmer. He's currently seventy-two and was a regional sales representative for an agricultural supply company during the time of the murders."

Kilmer's pictures captured a man with a more corporate appearance. He had a clean-shaven, oval face, framed by neatly combed dark hair that was just starting to recede at the temples. His eyes were dark and narrow, like a man always readying himself to confront some unseen threat.

"His job required frequent travel up and down the I-5 corridor and he matched a description of a possible suspect from the second murder. When questioned, he was found with three or four newspaper clippings about the case."

"The Interstate Reaper was one of the most sensational cases of the 1980s," Jack interjected. "*Everyone* was reading about it."

"He's not wrong," Violet said, "but in a case with little evidence, they were looking for anything they could get. Although Kilmer was questioned multiple times due to his proximity to several abduction sites, his alibis for the dates in question were generally solid. Lastly, there was Simon

Sanchez, younger than the rest. Now sixty-eight. He was a freelance photographer who often worked along I-5, capturing landscapes and cityscapes. He did some time after the last murder, an unrelated robbery."

Sanchez looked distinctly different from the other two. He was lean, with sharp cheekbones and a pointed chin that gave him a somewhat hawkish appearance. His hair was long and tied back in most of the photos, and he sported a sparse, scruffy beard. He was young at the time of the first murder and, if the pictures were an accurate representation, was always in a bad mood.

"He looks like someone who might grumble about *nuisances* while roaming around a campground," Jack said, leaning forward and looking more invested, for the moment.

"His presence near one of the locations where the third victim was last seen was troubling," Violet continued. "Plus, he had two arrests on his record that didn't end up getting prosecuted. One for drugs, where he got sent to a diversion program, and another for domestic violence against a girl-friend, a redhead. After the initial complaint, she withdrew the charge, changed her story."

"That sounds like a promising suspect," Claire said.

"Unfortunately," Violet replied, "no direct evidence has ever linked him to the crimes, and his lifestyle and lack of a fixed schedule made it difficult to track his movements accurately. He remains a person of interest, mainly due to his inconsistent accounts of his whereabouts on key dates."

Claire's phone vibrated with her alarm. "Time for me to go," she said, standing. She made eye contact with Kiko, then Fitz and Jack, then nodded at the back of Violet's head on her way across the room. "You four debate this, because I'm torn. It's a lot of work for probably little payoff, but if you can come to a 4-0 or 3-1 decision on where to start, I'll go along."

"If it's 2-2?" Fitz asked.

Claire looked over her shoulder as she opened the door. "If it's 2-2, I'll break the tie. Or maybe I'll let Ranger decide."

CHAPTER SIX

"WHAT ARE you most looking forward to learning?" Claire asked Benny as they got out of the taxi in front of the sleek modern building that housed Game Gem Studios.

She had made it to the ferry just as it pulled in, and had met Benny as he walked off. Or, rather, as he'd *swaggered* off the ferry, full of confidence and, she was beginning to worry, perhaps a bit of *over*confidence.

Although he'd been born with Down Syndrome, neither she nor he had ever let this get in the way of him pursuing his interests and dreams. This was an excellent thing, and Claire was thrilled with the recent success of his YouTube channel. But it came with worry, too. She knew how cruel the internet could be, and she knew that steep ascents often came with rough descents. Not only that, but she'd seen success go to people's heads. And when Benny had been contacted out of the blue by Game Gem Studios, his normal confidence had increased into something bordering on cockiness.

That's why she had asked the question. She hoped he was still humble enough to want to learn.

Benny stared up at the building's impressive glass facade. "I just want to see how it all works, mom. I see all the games from a player's point of view. I want to see them from a creator's point of view."

"And this is the company that makes all of the games you trained on a few years back?"

He nodded.

Benny's school had introduced him to a suite of video games designed to help with short-term memory and other issues that sometimes came along with Down Syndrome. To Claire, they had been a godsend, and she had even used some of them herself. Her memory wasn't what it was in her twenties or thirties, and the games were accessible to all sorts of people. Unlike many video games, they had specific functions designed to help people grow and achieve more.

"Just remember," she said as they entered the lobby, "ask questions and listen, okay?"

"Got it, mom." He stopped and looked up at her. He was growing fast but hadn't hit the huge growth spurt she expected to begin at any minute, and she still had about six inches on him. "Don't worry, I'm no gamer-god or anything. Just don't tell anybody I still like to play *Fish Wars II* with my mom." He winked at her and this put her at ease.

At least he could still joke about himself.

Inside, Claire trailed behind Benny as Thera, the company representative with bright purple hair and more facial piercings than Claire could count, led them through the bustling corridors of the company's headquarters. Though distracted by her cellphone's constant buzzing in her pocket, she could still feel the excitement, creativity, and youthful energy of the place. There was something infectious about it, and she could see the excitement on her son's face.

Pausing in the stairwell as Thera led Benny to another floor, she pulled out her phone. She had a new text from Fitz.

All five of the murders line up with openings of Sunny Skillet diners within a couple hundred miles of the crime scene. Gus Cunningham was in the area for EVERY SINGLE MURDER.

Claire considered this. A couple hundred miles was hardly "in the area," but it was something, at least.

She continued reading the text.

We can't find travel logs, but Violet is working on it. If she can't find it, I may have to visit the restaurants in person. Think Rivera would approve a $500 chicken-and-waffles expenditure? Anyway, the current vote is 2-2.

When they reached the second floor, Claire glanced around, taking in the open-plan offices, quite a contrast to the cramped, windowless Boiler Room. Computer monitors flickered with lines of code while groups of developers huddled together, some chatting seriously, some laughing. The walls were adorned with concept art and posters of popular games, adding a splash of color to the otherwise industrial décor. Her twin girls, both in college, had showed no interest in computers or technology as professions, but she wondered whether Benny would end up working in a place like this.

Thera paused to explain the company's workflow and Benny listened intently, his eyes wide with wonder. Despite the fact that her phone had buzzed in her pocket yet again, Claire smiled, watching her son's enthusiasm ignite.

As they continued the tour, Claire read the new text from Fitz.

Jack thinks a couple of the original suspects may be worth looking into. Thinks he can solve the cold case by sheer power of his biceps or something. Still 2-2.

Thera led them into a large room marked "Game Testing," where rows of computers lined bright pink walls. Claire tuned out the conversation as she received another text, but Benny's curiosity seemed boundless as he peppered Thera with questions about the testing process.

Kiko and Jack seem to be getting on the same page. They both like the angle of previous suspects, which is fine by me as long as I get a crack at Cunningham. We are approaching a 4-0 vote, methinks. By the way, I believe Kiko and Jack are getting in the same *bed* as well.

Their tour concluded in the company's break room, the aroma of freshly brewed coffee mingling with the sound of laughter and animated conversation.

"And that brings us to you, Benny," Thera said.

Claire put her phone away.

Benny's face was bright red, as it often got while he was actively gaming or otherwise excited about something. "This is great."

Thera laughed. "Yes it is, and so is your channel. We want to offer you exclusive early access to our next line of games. You'll get them two weeks before anyone else, you can give us feedback, play them, review them on your channel, whatever you want."

Benny shot a look at Claire, then his face grew serious. "And what's in it for me?" He folded his arms and frowned.

Thera cast a surprised look at Claire, as though asking, *is this kid for real?*

"In terms of compensation, I mean," Benny continued. "What are we looking at here?"

Claire knew this routine. Benny was always full of jokes, and he'd learned that sometimes the best joke of all was pretending to be rigidly serious and businesslike.

After a long, awkward silence, he cracked a smile. "Just kidding," he said. "You know I'm in."

On their way downstairs in the elevator, Claire pulled out her phone one more time. Fitz had texted again.

4-0. We're going after the Interstate Reaper. Meet at Evergreen at 10 AM?

CHAPTER SEVEN

THE LATE MORNING was warm and pungent. An overnight rain had dislodged layers of filth and organics from the parking lot, and now the sun bore into the asphalt producing steam with a mossy, urban scent.

Still, Claire thought, there was something pleasant about this particular facility. Well-groomed trees dotted the dividers in the parking lot, which had a layer of fresh mulch, indicating to Claire that this was one of the higher-end memory care facilities.

The facade, interspersed with large windows, appeared well-kept, the brick walls a rich red-brown against the pale blue sky. Small, colorful flower beds lined the walkway, their blooms flourishing despite the frequent drizzles typical of the area.

Reaching the front door, Claire heard the gurgle of a small electric waterfall, which gave the lobby a calming, almost spa-like atmosphere. An ambiance that was quickly destroyed by the sound of Fitz and Jack coming around the corner.

"I told you to let *me* drive," Jack was saying. "I mean, are you sure you have driven in this country before, or *any* country for that matter? Do you even have a driver's license, Fitz?"

"That guy came out of nowhere," Fitz said. "And we're all lucky I was paying as much attention as I was. Missed him by half a meter!"

Claire rounded the corner and stopped when she saw them. They weren't alone. A tall man, roughly fifty years old, was walking behind them, smiling as if entertained by their banter. He was clearly part of the staff as he wore a long white medical coat and walked with an air of importance.

"Claire," Fitz called from a few paces away, "how the hell are you?"

Claire ignored this and shook the man's hand as they stopped and moved up against the hallway wall.

"Chris Thacker, GNP and Executive Director," the man said, holding her hand just a fraction of a second longer than she'd expected.

"Special Agent in Charge, Claire Anderson."

Thacker had the build of a man more accustomed to hiking through rough terrain than walking medical facility corridors; his broad shoulders filled out a lab coat that seemed at odds with his naturally imposing stature. "I'm *hoping* these two are with you. I'm not expecting any admissions today..." he gestured at Jack and Fitz... "but I can give you a clinical recommendation for their ongoing care needs."

Claire laughed. "I'd appreciate that. The care burden these two place on me is considerable." Claire saw Kiko, running up behind them. "She's with us as well."

"Your colleagues were briefly filling me in on the situation," Thacker said, growing serious. "Follow me into my office and I can tell you more about the patient."

Claire followed Thacker down the hallway, trailed by the others. Apparently, Claire's presence or Thacker's jokes had shamed the men into ceasing their bickering.

He led them into a large office and offered Claire one of the two chairs. He sat in the other behind his desk as Fitz, Kiko, and Jack hugged the wall.

"I don't know all the details, and I'm sure you understand I can't say everything. But in the year since Mr. Cunningham became a part of our facility, he has been presenting with the common symptoms of vascular dementia. His acute episodic memory loss and impaired reasoning are predominant. At ninety years old, his journey with this condition has been marked by fluctuating periods of clarity, but he's most often found in a state of confusion that sometimes leads to agitation. His medical history of hypertension and previous strokes are contributing factors. The care team's efforts are concentrated on stabilizing his emotional fluctuations and providing a structured routine that helps mitigate his outbursts. Mr. Cunningham's physical health remains stable, with personalized care plans in place to address both his cognitive challenges and physical wellbeing."

"That was the clinical version," Claire said, "and I appreciate it. But can you just level with us a bit? What's he like?"

Thacker had a faint scar on his left cheek, which he rubbed unconsciously, the only tic of nervousness in his otherwise calm demeanor. "I'm not entirely sure how solid the ground is on which I'm standing," he said. "There are HIPAA regulations to think about, and this all happened very quickly."

"The CNA," Claire asked, "Lydia Ramirez. How is she doing?"

"We take every incident of patient-staff aggression seriously even when, as in this case, no serious harm was done.

She was very upset that we made her take a few paid days off to recover."

"Did you have any inkling of anything strange about this man?" Claire asked.

"Not at all," Thacker said. "Many of our patients exhibit what might be considered strange behavior to those who do not understand memory loss, Alzheimer's, and other types of dementia. These conditions manifest differently in different patients."

Claire was intent on breaking through his clinical veneer. She cocked her head slightly and offered a warm smile, which was easy given his three-day stubble and handsome looks. "Doctor Thacker," she said, then she stopped herself and turned to Jack, Fitz, and Kiko. "Can you give me a second?"

She nodded toward the door and held Jack's gaze until he led the other three out.

When the door clicked shut behind them, she turned back to him. "Doctor Thacker—"

"It's actually not 'Doctor.' I'm a GNP, Geriatric Nurse Practitioner. Also got a Master's in Business Admin because I knew I wanted to run a place just like this one day."

She smiled. "My apologies. Just between us, off the record, answer two things for me. First, is Mr. Cunningham's condition such that he would be compelled to share old memories he's been hiding for his entire life? Or is it more likely that he could be confusing things he read about with things he did?"

"Yes," Thacker said.

"What do you mean, 'yes'?" Claire asked.

"I mean that both are equally likely given his condition, and I have no idea which it is. I wish I could help you, and I would if I could, but I truly don't know."

"Then on to my second question," Claire said. "Is he dangerous right now?"

"As I said to Agent Russo when he called to set up this meeting, he is not dangerous. He is a frail ninety-year-old man and, though he has moments of lucidity, he is genuinely confused about most things most of the time." Thacker shook his head sadly. "That's the case with most of our patients. Although I always recommend caution, no, I do not think he is dangerous in any way."

He stood, indicating to Claire that he didn't want to say much more. And that was fine by her.

She was about to meet Augustus Cunningham face to face and, as someone who prided herself on having pretty good gut instincts, she was fascinated by what the meeting would tell her.

CHAPTER EIGHT

"KNOCK, KNOCK, MR. CUNNINGHAM?" The moment the nurse opened the door and leaned into Augustus Cunningham's room, Claire knew it was too small for all of them.

Cunningham sat in a wheelchair in the corner, staring out the window, his legs covered by what looked to be a homemade Afghan, his hands folded atop it. The blanket was white and green, with little yellow flowers, and it reminded Claire of one she'd inherited from her uncle when he'd passed away.

"Knock, knock," the nurse repeated. "Mr. Cunningham?"

Cunningham didn't look over as the nurse entered, didn't look up as Fitz strolled right in after her. Just sat, nearly motionless, hands folded in his lap.

Claire took the opportunity to address Jack and Kiko. "This is going to be overwhelming for him if we are all here," she said. "Can you two wait outside?"

Jack folded his arms and stared Claire down for a good couple of seconds before Kiko flashed a smile. "I skipped breakfast. Come on, Jack, I know you don't eat candy for breakfast, but I think I saw some beef jerky in the vending machines."

Kiko pulled him out the door as the nurse squatted next to the wheelchair to reach Cunningham's eye level and spoke. "Gus, you have some visitors who would like to ask you a few questions. Will that be alright?"

Cunningham slowly turned toward them. Claire didn't know if what she saw in his eyes was confusion, fatigue, or something else entirely. He nodded almost imperceptibly. "Okay," was all he said.

"Mr. Cunningham," Claire spoke in a gentle voice as the nurse withdrew. "I'm Claire Anderson and this is Fitz Pembroke—"

"The Third," Fitz interjected.

Claire had agreed to let Fitz take the lead, and he'd convinced her that they shouldn't lead with a request to record his voice or take a DNA sample. First of all, he'd argued, it would almost certainly terrify him. And second, it wouldn't hold up unless they either got a court order, which would take days, or Cunningham gave them explicit consent, which he was not mentally coherent enough to do.

Although Claire was no psychologist herself, she had conducted her fair share of interviews, and in a case like this, she knew Fitz would follow a five-step process.

First, establish rapport. Second, gently probe for details of the crime or the historical period during which the crime took place. The third piece, at least as she'd learned it, was called *presenting ephemera*—photographs, magazines, concert tickets, old clothing, anything that might trigger a memory. All they had in that camp were crime scene photos and the audio clip. Fourth, without directly linking him to any crimes, Fitz would introduce details from the case file to see what response they generated. Finally, if the situation warranted it, there would be a more direct confrontation.

All the while, of course, both Fitz and Claire would be observing Cunningham for behavioral cues. Although, in a suspect whose memory was fading and unreliable, that became much more difficult.

As the nurse shut the door behind her, Fitz began, and Claire noticed that he skipped straight to the issue of ephemera because Cunningham had reached for a photo book that had been sitting on the windowsill. He was now thumbing through it absent-mindedly, but not looking down at the photos.

Fitz moved to Cunningham's side and briefly attempted to squat as the nurse had. Opting not to test the resiliency of his knees, he instead leaned forward with his hands behind his back and looked at the photos over the man's shoulder, as though he was a family member reminiscing about days gone by.

"Who's that one?" Fitz asked.

Cunningham ignored him and flipped the page.

"And what about her?"

Claire stood on the other side of the room and could see that the photographs were the sort of faded colors typical of photos from the 1960s and 1970s.

"Susan Kelly," Cunningham said, touching one of the photographs with a long, bony finger. His voice sounded nothing like the man in the audio clip, although that didn't mean much. While the man on the clip had sounded aggressive and wicked, Cunningham's voice now was weak and confused.

Fitz smiled. "Did she work at the Sunny Skillet Diner? One of the ones you helped open?"

Cunningham looked up at Fitz and seemed genuinely surprised that the man knew something of his background.

Cunningham nodded. "Portland," he said, "or Seattle."
His eyes were searching.

"1961. No, 1971. Oh, hmmm..." He shook his head and frowned as though the memory had slipped away.

There was no acting in him. Claire knew what real confusion looked like, and this was it. Heck, Claire could barely remember what year she had gotten married half of the time, and she was half his age.

Cunningham folded the photo book closed when he got to a series of empty pages.

Fitz sat on a small plastic chair opposite him. Claire flinched as the chair wobbled slightly under his large frame. She guessed it was built for people under two hundred pounds, but it seemed ready to hold up, just barely.

"Portland and Seattle," Fitz said. "You worked all up and down Interstate 5, the whole area from California all the way up nearly to Canada. Must have been an exciting job. All of that travel?"

Cunningham looked at Fitz, then glanced at Claire. His pale, wrinkled flesh sagged off his narrow, bony face, almost like it was trying to escape. "Who are you?"

"Claire Anderson," Claire said, a little more condescendingly than she wished. "We'd like to ask some questions about the past, if you don't mind."

"The past is gone," Cunningham said, "but we forget nothing."

"What kind of things do you remember from that time?" Fitz asked pleasantly, but he didn't give the man a chance to answer. "Personally, I wasn't alive then, but I wish I had been. The sixties and seventies in America. A golden age. Across the pond, we had the Beatles. But here, well, you know, it was a great time for a man in their prime to be alive, right Mr. Cunningham?"

Cunningham looked out the window. "Time," he said. "A great time, I believe."

"Were you ever married during that time?" Fitz asked.

Cunningham didn't respond.

"Any children?" Fitz continued. "I don't have any of my own. And, truth be told, I'd be a rubbish father."

"Married," Cunningham said. "Are you married to her?" He moved his head slightly, indicating Claire.

Fitz let out a short burst of laughter. "Who? Agent Anderson here? As much as being married to me would tickle her biscuits, no. She *has* pursued me for years, but I am a loner. A *sigma*, as the kids these days say."

Claire rolled her eyes, but said nothing. If this was his idea of building rapport, it wasn't working.

"Nah, I'm just kidding," Fitz said.

He went quiet as Cunningham slowly turned to face him.

"Always had a thing for redheads myself," Fitz continued. "Irish ladies especially. Do you know any red-headed women? Someone from your past or maybe a nurse who works here?"

Cunningham's eyes, which had been vague and distant, sharpened suddenly. His hands gripped the arms of his wheelchair, knuckles whitening. A flush crept up his neck, and his voice was a hoarse whisper. "Why do you keep asking me about that?"

Fitz cocked his head. "I only asked it once, good sir."

"Everyone always with the redheads."

"What about it, Gus? Do you recall a red headed nurse? She serves you your milktoast?"

"Where's my breakfast?" Cunningham hissed.

Claire sensed the rising tension. She had noted a subtle shift in Cunningham's demeanor, an agitation that seemed to swell with the last few questions. The room felt smaller, the atmosphere charged with an intensity that was too much for the fragile balance they were trying to maintain. It was clear that Cunningham was no longer merely confused, but was teetering on the edge of distress.

Fitz may have noted the same, but he didn't care. Instead, he leaned in aggressively, the small plastic chair creaking beneath him. "Any redheads in your photo book?" He reached for it, but Cunningham swatted at his hand, a more aggressive movement than Claire had thought him capable of.

"Alright, Fitz, that's enough," Claire said sharply, her voice cutting through the tension. "We're not here to cause distress." She stepped closer to Cunningham, kneeling as the nurse had, her expression softening. "Mr. Cunningham, I'm sorry. We don't need to continue this right now."

Fitz looked at her, a flicker of protest in his eyes, but Claire got him out of the chair with her look.

"Breakfast," Cunningham said, his mind apparently still on the milktoast despite the fact that breakfast had ended a couple hours earlier. "I want my breakfast."

CHAPTER NINE

"FITZ, he's ninety some years old, and has high blood pressure," Claire said as she led Fitz down the hallway. "This guy is Silent Generation era. You can't pressure him into a confession like some stoned Gen Xer you already know is guilty."

"You're right," Fitz admitted. "I could feel his blood pressure spiking, and I should've backed off sooner. We can't prosecute him if he's dead."

They found Kiko and Jack sitting at a small table in an informal dining and lounge area. Claire figured it was designed so that visitors could take their family members for a semi-private visit, but still be within emergency medication dispensing range of the nurse. Judging by the little flier taped to the wall, it was also the site of Evergreen's weekly bingo night.

Jack slid an empty beef jerky bag back and forth on the table, looking more frustrated than he had when Claire had kicked him out of the interview before it started.

Kiko, on the other hand, seemed to be having an engaging conversation with three women who sat at a table next to them, a deck of cards in front of each of them. "This is Sister Ruth, Sister Veronica, and Sister Ella," Kiko said, as though introducing old friends.

Only Sister Ruth looked up. The others just sat there, eyes on the table.

"We have been discussing the facility," Kiko said, "and Sister Ella tells me that they have delicious breakfast every morning."

Fitz took a seat next to Jack and examined the empty beef jerky package. Turning to Kiko, he asked, "Would you be an absolute diamond and spare me some of that vending machine candy that you were speaking of?"

Kiko shook her head, "None left."

"How did the interview with Cunningham go?" Jack asked Claire, purposefully ignoring Fitz even though, of course, he knew that Fitz had led the interview.

"Gus." Sister Ella spat on the ground and, clenching her fists, she started to shake. "*Così l'animale perverso vidi.*" She spoke through clenched teeth, her wrinkled forehead tensing.

"*Va bene, va bene.*" Jack knelt next to the woman, holding her hands and speaking softly. "*Parlo italiano, nonna.*"

The women all looked at Jack, somewhat stunned. Claire knew he spoke many languages but, in general, Jack was a man of few words.

Sister Ella looked into Jack's eyes and calmed quickly, but said nothing. She smiled, then patted him on the cheek as though he was her own grandson.

"What did she say about Gus?" Claire asked.

Fitz was quick to interject before Jack could respond. "It depends on the translation of Dante you happen to favor, but essentially it means, *Thus I saw the perverse animal.* She's quoting *The Divine Comedy.*"

Claire considered this. "Say more."

She regretted it almost immediately because, when asked to elaborate, especially on a scholarly subject, Fitz was only *too* eager to do so.

"On his journey through hell, Dante encounters terrible creatures that try to block his path to enlightenment. Sins and moral failings are represented symbolically. A she-wolf —the 'perverse animal'—not only embodies the specific sins of avarice and incontinence, but also mirrors broader societal corruption. The grotesque transformation of a soul that engages willingly in malevolent deeds is a core theme of the *Inferno*. This genius, a bloke after my own heart, pointed his accusatory finger far and wide. Absolute bloody brilliance. I could go on," Fitz warned, "but I sense your boredom."

"Jack," Claire said, shifting focus, "ask her what she knows about Cunningham."

"My Italian isn't as good as it used to be, but I'll give it a shot."

Jack launched into a long question, occasionally searching for a word but sounding better at Italian than Claire herself had ever been at any language. As he spoke, Claire watched the expression on Sister Ella's face darken.

When he'd finished, Sister Ella looked at Claire. "*Così l'animale perverso vidi.*"

"Can you say a little more?" Claire asked, recognizing the same phrase she had used before.

Sister Ella reached for the deck of cards and opened the pack, then seemed to lose interest and set them down. "*È molto cattivo. Lui ha un inferno dentro di sé.*"

Jack looked at Claire. "*He is very bad*, she says. *He has a hell inside him.*"

~

Fitz paused in the doorway of the Boiler Room and stared in at Claire, who had already taken her usual seat around the table. *"Lasciate ogni speranza,"* he said in a poor Italian accent, *"voi ch'entrate."*

"Abandon all hope, ye who enter here," Violet called from the corner. "And yes, I do that every time I come to work, but why risk indigestion quoting Dante before lunch?"

Everyone took their seats around the table, and Claire reached down to scratch Ranger behind his ears. Over the last few weeks, their golden retriever had slowly learned that, while Fitz was freer with the treats and more likely to share his lunch, Claire provided a steady and consistent presence that he seemed to welcome. In general, Ranger would check to see if Fitz had any food and then camp out with Claire. And she didn't mind. As much as he seemed to be calmed by her gentle hand, she found his presence calming as well.

"Fitz," Claire said, "give everyone the quick summary."

Fitz cleared his throat. "The GNP's diagnosis was, surprisingly, correct."

"Wait," Claire said, "why did you say 'surprisingly'?"

"Didn't care for the fellow, that's all." He cleared his throat. "In any case, Augustus Cunningham is suffering from acute memory loss and confusion. But the way he grew agitated around the question of redheads tells me that the nurse—umm, Lydia, was it?—was onto something. I wish I could say with more certainty, but I honestly don't know if he is the killer or if he is just someone who becomes agitated when thinking about redheads. It's possible he knows something about it but isn't himself guilty. As much as I'd like to say that his agitation is clearly a sign of guilt, his mind is not a normal mind and there are just too many variables."

Jack said, "I still can't believe I agreed to spend time on this. There are dozens of killers out there right now harming our community. Fentanyl is coming in through the ports and through the northern border. All sorts of crap is going down all around our city, and we are spending time talking to a ninety-year-old guy who is clearly no threat in the present day." He shook his head.

Claire said, "You voted to pursue this yesterday. Why the change?"

Jack didn't answer, and she figured it was because he hadn't been allowed in the interview.

"Don't worry, Jack. Next you can pursue the previous suspects. See if you can prove Lydia wrong. And Violet," Claire continued, "did you get anything else about his past?"

"Hold on," Violet said, "I'll have something in a moment."

Fitz was staring daggers at Jack. "Everyone deserves justice. Even people who passed away forty or fifty years ago."

"Is that really why you are into this case?" Jack asked, "or is it because, to you, cases and human minds are just puzzles to be put together? I don't think you actually care about protecting people or the community. You just care about being right."

A faint smile cracked across Fitz's face. "Being right, yes, and being smarter than everyone else."

Kiko broke their back and forth. "Jack, why are you always trying to tear Fitz down?"

"No, no," Fitz said. "Jack's actually onto something. He's right that I have never connected to this work because I actually care about other people. And I certainly don't have some rigorous moral code. But as long as I'm *smart* and *right*, this work will continue to value me. And as long as the FBI wants to pay me to stand around being smart and right, the work is valuable to me. I'm fine with leaving the caring to people with a constitution for warmth."

Jack shook his head, unable to conjure a response.

Claire pressed her hands into the table. "Team," she said, "we need to figure out where we are going to go from here."

"I know where we're going." Light bounced off the back of Violet's head, her silken black hair animated by the subtle movements made from speaking.

"Where's that?" Claire asked.

Violet swiveled around in her desk chair. "You know how Jonathan wouldn't approve the hardware and software I wanted?"

Claire nodded.

"I kinda rigged my own thing. We are going to go back to the scenes of the crimes."

"What?" Claire asked.

"Back in time. Starting with 1979."

CHAPTER TEN

"WHAT DO YOU MEAN, 'go back in time'?" Claire asked.

Violet ignored her and plugged a thick black cable into the back of one of her monitors. Claire saw that the cable ran to a strap-on headset that sat between two empty bags of potato chips on her desk. Claire couldn't help but wonder where that headset had come from, how much it had cost, and what sort of scenario funded its purchase. If it had cost ten grand and had come from a clandestine Israeli tech firm, it wouldn't shock her. As head of the detachment, it was Claire's job to know every facet of her team's activity, but she intentionally chose to ignore her questions for the time being.

Violet tapped a button, and the large monitor on the wall flickered to life. It showed a scene from the 1970s, and Claire knew right away that it was the crime scene from the first murder in Bellingham, Washington.

Violet walked over to Claire, holding the headset. "Stand up and strap this on."

"What is it?" Claire asked.

"Your son Benny is into video games, right?" Violet replied. "Maybe he has one of these VR headsets."

"I know he's been asking about getting one, but they are fairly expensive."

"Like most gaming systems, when other companies catch on and come out with a clone product, the price drops drastically. They're down to around three or four hundred dollars now." Violet looked down to adjust the straps. "Well, most of them are," she said under her breath.

"And this one?" Claire couldn't stop herself from asking.

"Well, okay, this one cost quite a bit more than that."

"I'm sure it did," Claire frowned.

On their first case together, Violet had used a stash of stolen bitcoin to buy a supercomputer that had helped crack the case before being returned to avoid various legal complications. Violet had been ordered not to request that any of the ill-gotten cryptocurrency be returned, though Claire wouldn't have been shocked if she'd found some way around that.

"As you're about to see," Violet said, "this headset is lightyears beyond most."

"What does it do?"

"I started by gathering all the old crime scene photos, dusty sketches, and any available videos or reports, then digitized them if they weren't already in a format I could use." Usually fairly apathetic, Violet's eyes lit up. "Next, I dove into this 3D modeling software—pretty cutting-edge stuff—to construct the scene from the ground up using modern images from Google Earth. It's like building a virtual diorama, except you're using photogrammetry techniques to transform those two-dimensional images into a fully navigable 3D space." She leaned in, enthusiasm undimmed. "Photogrammetry is the real game-changer. It lets us create precise 3D replicas from flat photos, which means that each object—from furniture down to small bloodstains—gets modeled in three dimensions. Then, I stitched those models into the broader environment I built, ensuring everything was to scale and in its rightful place, just as it was back in the seventies or eighties." Pausing for effect, she continued, "Then I integrated the whole shebang into a VR platform, adding interactive elements so you can actually 'walk' through the scene, interact with objects— maybe lift a cup to see the ring it left on the table, stuff like that. And after running advanced lighting simulations, I recreated the exact conditions based on the time of day the photos were taken."

Violet lifted the headset and Claire dipped her head to allow her to set it over her eyes and adjust the straps. Claire opened her eyes to visuals that placed her in the center of a slowly morphing three dimensional blue and purple meditation mandala.

"What you're seeing now are just the images I threw together to prevent screen burn. The system is advanced, but the monitor is very sensitive."

Claire didn't want to let Violet know how impressed she was with the system for fear she would find a way to blow their miniscule budget on the next big tech thing. Or worse, find a way to fund it using a questionable source. She *did* wish Benny were here to take a look.

"I peppered the scene with hotspots," Violet continued. "Trigger them, and you get detailed info, zoom-in capabilities, even embedded audio clips where available. It's all about making this as immersive and informative as possible. You're literally stepping into a moment frozen in time, equipped with the tech to peel back layers nobody's seen in decades. It's part forensics, part time travel. Ready?"

Claire nodded.

"The others will all be watching a 2D version of what

you're seeing, a wide angle view as though looking through a spyhole lens."

Inside the headset, the light dimmed until the mandala disappeared. All of a sudden, Claire was fully immersed in the crime scene in a way she hadn't thought possible.

She found herself standing on a pebbly beach and saw the beautiful, still waters of Puget Sound, and in the distance, snow capped mountains. She knew instantly that she was at the first crime scene in Bellingham, Washington.

The victim had been found dead in some brambles on a small beach about a mile from downtown. Turning away from the water to where trees and brambles stood in a line at the base of a large embankment, Claire tried to maintain her balance. She heard the sound of pebbles clacking together under her feet as she moved. Glancing up, she saw a few houses perched at the top of the embankment and staring out at the water.

Violet's voice interrupted the scene. "I don't yet have it set up so you can walk around the scene," she said. "Just stand still, and I will walk you through it from my keyboard."

Claire nearly toppled over as she felt herself walking forward inside the scene, her perspective jarred. From the keyboard, Violet was controlling the point of view as though Claire was walking up a slight slope toward the brambles. Then, it was as though Claire herself had crouched to get a better look. The view zoomed in and Claire saw the body. The victim had been positioned sitting cross-legged amidst the leaves, head tilted back, her gray pants and white shirt both flecked with mud and dirt.

In the crime scene photograph she'd seen, the victim had been lying under a sheet, but Claire now assumed that it had been taken well after the initial discovery of the body. "Is this the position she was in upon discovery?"

"That's right," Violet replied.

The perspective zoomed in even further, and Claire could see that the victim's head was pointed out at the water and the mountains beyond. She had clear ligature marks around her neck that matched Claire's understanding that the manner of death had been strangulation.

"From what I've gathered," Fitz said, his voice an odd interruption, "these murders were about power, control, sadism, even hatred of women. It's entirely possible this man was just born this way, but it is more likely that he suffered from a cruel mother or other female relative. The files state that there was evidence to believe he had them tied up for multiple hours before killing them. But with no evidence of sexual assault or torture, it makes one wonder what he was doing during those hours. It's an abnormal MO. My guess? He was talking to them, possibly seeking forgiveness or possibly seeking vengeance verbally. The strangulations were all efficient, neat, and clean. No blood. No torture, no signs of malice."

"No signs of malice save for the *murderous strangulation*," Kiko corrected.

Claire tilted her head to get a look at the woman's face. Her eyes were vacant and glassy, and the fact that her head was pointed toward the water, the beautiful view of Puget Sound and the mountains in the distance, made Claire's heart twist.

She took off the headset and looked at Violet. "That was disconcerting on so many levels."

CHAPTER ELEVEN

OVER THE NEXT TWO HOURS, Claire visited the other four crime scenes, each more unsettling than the last. Looking at photographs was bad enough, but Violet had truly created an immersive experience that, while not technologically perfect, was much more immersive than Claire had expected.

As much as she'd wanted to rip off the headset with each new corpse, she felt she owed it to the women to be on the scene where they had been found. The second victim was named Francis Graber. Abducted from a bus stop in Grants Pass, Oregon, her body had been found about thirty yards from the Rogue River in a small park three days later. The crime scene that Violet was able to put together was not quite as realized as the first one because photos from the time had not been taken from as many different angles. She had filled in some with modern photos, but some of the landscape had changed, causing a few incongruities in Claire's view of the scene. Still, seeing Francis Graber rendered in 3D, with ligature marks that matched the first victim, chilled Claire to the bone.

Next she traveled to Portland, Oregon, a case that was slightly different. Pamela Crane—who had been arrested for possession of drugs multiple times and was said to score heroin on the corner of Southeast 82nd Street—was abducted late on a Friday night. Her body was discovered Sunday morning near Crystal Springs Lake, not far from Reed College, right in the city. As Claire had crouched down to inspect her in the 3D world, she'd noted that Crane had some bruising on her face, though it wasn't clear what had caused it. The first two victims had been found in more remote locations, but Crane's body had been dumped near a well-known college, indicating that the killer may have become more willing to risk exposure as he went along.

The next scene Claire knew well. It was Discovery Park in Seattle, and the victim's name was Caroline Smith. Smith was said to have taken frequent walks in the park and had been abducted there and found two days later in a little area of wetlands called the Utah Wetlands.

Claire had walked there herself and, as she turned, headset on, and examined the scene, she felt more than ever like Caroline Smith's fate could have been hers.

After two murders in major cities, the killer returned to a more remote area for his final known murder in 1989.

Claire could feel the dust of Yreka, California as she entered the scene overlooking the Klamath River. She knew from the case files that it had been over a hundred degrees that day in August and, as she examined the body of Susan Swanson, cross-legged and leaning on a thin tree, she felt sick to her stomach.

When Violet piped in the chilling audio—*You little nuisance*—Claire knew she'd had enough.

Some agents developed detachment, but Claire wasn't like that. She was personally affected by each and every one of these cases and would never abandon the position that this was a *good* thing. She took it personally and that made her better at the job.

As she pulled off the headset, she blinked rapidly and looked around the room. She had almost forgotten that the rest of her crew were present as well, watching a 2D rendering on the large screen. She was fairly sure they'd picked up many of the same details she had, though she doubted they had the same felt sense of the scene.

Both Fitz and Jack looked eager to speak, and she held up a single finger to stop them. Something in her gut told her she wanted to hear from Kiko. Claire had noticed something that wasn't mentioned in the files, and she wanted to know if Kiko, the youngest member of the team and only two weeks past her probationary period, had noticed it as well.

Nodding in her direction, Claire said, "Kiko, I don't want you to feel like the new kid in class who gets picked on by the teacher, but I'm interested, what did you notice?"

Kiko stood and paced, looking like she was about to speak. Then she saw Ranger eyeing her from the corner and sat down again, inching her chair in the other direction.

Claire found it funny that Kiko didn't like animals, even dogs. Or maybe it wasn't that she didn't *like* them, but she certainly wasn't comfortable with them, having grown up without much contact with animals.

Kiko's face, usually bright and enthusiastic, was dark, even grim. "In the theater world, we are taught that every choice we make with our bodies, with our words, with our inflections, matters. One time I was rehearsing a scene for a play, *A Raisin in the Sun*, I think, and the director could tell I was phoning it in. Just kind of going through it without making clear decisions about the character. He called me out on it. And he was right." She paused, considering her next words carefully. "My sense is that our killer is very thoughtful. Not thoughtful in the sense that he'll bring you flowers and candy on Valentine's Day and remember your favorite drink order at Starbucks. Thoughtful in the sense that he did things deliberately. I'm not an expert in crime scene investigation, but the strangulation marks were all very consistent, and that is over a ten-year period, at least. There could of course be other murders that haven't yet been linked. Obviously, the locations are consistent along the I-5 corridor. But there's something else..."

Claire held up a full hand to stop Jack and Fitz from interrupting.

"The water," Kiko said. "All five bodies were found near water, which was in the case file, but it's not only that. Each of the bodies seemed staged somehow. Placed in an exact way. The killer made choices about how he left the bodies. He was very deliberate with it. Almost as though he'd wanted them to have a nice view after death."

"Exactly," Claire said, proud that Kiko had picked up on the same thing she had. "Did anyone else notice that they were all *facing* the water?"

She glanced toward Jack and Fitz, then nodded at Jack.

"I noticed that as well," Jack said. "Seems like a potential coincidence."

Fitz shook his head definitively. "A coincidence? Over a ten-year period? That five out of five women would be found dead near a body of water and facing that body of water, all sitting either cross-legged or in some other way hunched against a tree or something? Not a coincidence. And if I may say so, it makes my psychological diagnosis quite a bit more solid. He wanted to control these women even after their deaths, and I'd bet anything that the water itself is significant in some way and the fact that they are looking at it is *also* significant."

"I think this is enough to revisit Mr. Augustus Cunningham," Claire said. "Maybe he's calmed down a bit and has something to say about water." From the corner of her eye, she noticed that Jack looked frustrated. "What?"

"Maybe there *is* something to all this," he said. "The controlling of women and the bodies of water and all that. I still think we would be better served by going back through the evidence we have rather than trying to pluck nuggets from a deteriorating mind. But that's not my call."

"What are you getting at, Jack?" Claire was frustrated. For a guy who thought of himself as an alpha, he could be pretty damn indirect sometimes.

"Let me and Kiko go interview Stacy Wegman," he said. "She was the lead agent on this case for ten years. Retired now, but she knows more about this case than anyone. Damn well sure she knows a lot that *isn't* in the files. You know I'm not going to be of any help at the memory care facility anyway."

Claire couldn't disagree. Jack wouldn't be much help at the memory care facility. She didn't even want Jack or Kiko in the room because it might overwhelm Cunningham. But she had some trepidation about letting Jack go on his own, especially with Kiko.

Still, she felt her head nodding in the affirmative. "Okay," she said. "Let's regroup here first thing tomorrow morning."

CHAPTER TWELVE

TO GET BACK to the memory care facility, Claire had to steal a car.

Jack and Kiko had left first, taking the only Suburban they were allowed to use. So Claire had called in a favor from the FBI's mechanic, who had just finished work on an older model sedan. She had nabbed it before he could even put it back into official circulation.

And it seemed as though the mechanic hadn't done much of a job because, by the time they parked, the heating gauge was showing that the engine was too hot to continue driving.

This pissed off Claire to no end, but Fitz didn't seem to care. "Sometimes things don't work, Claire," he said as he got out of the car. "You'd have a lot more fun in life if you accepted that not everything has to be perfect."

She followed him across the parking lot and he held the door open for her as they walked in.

"Thank you, Doctor Phil," she said, frowning at him.

Fitz lurched back and held his heart as though he'd been struck with an arrow. "I could have accepted Doctor

Freud or Jung or even Phil Donahue, though he's not a doctor. Do you really equate me with that dime-store celebrity shrink?"

Claire didn't answer because, now in the lobby, she spied the nurse who'd started this whole thing a few days earlier. Lydia Ramirez was pushing a med cart down the hall and Claire hurried after her. "Lydia!"

The nurse turned and dropped her eyes the moment she recognized Claire.

"How are you doing?" Claire asked. "Are you feeling any better?"

Lydia looked left and right and made her voice a hushed whisper. "Feeling any better that I am working in a building that houses—essentially working *for*—a serial killer? Yeah, I feel just amazing about that." Then, catching herself, she added, "I'm sorry. I don't mean to be sarcastic. I thought you guys would have arrested him by now, or, I don't know, *something*."

"I'm sorry. It doesn't work that way."

Lydia sighed. "Look, I'm thankful you're here, but I think you can understand that I'm not willing to go back in that guy's room."

Claire nodded. "Absolutely."

She heard Fitz's lumbering steps coming up behind her, and she expected him to stop and say something he thought was brilliant to Lydia. But he didn't. Instead, he headed straight for Cunningham's door.

This was Fitz's Super Bowl, birthday, and Christmas all rolled into one, she realized. With no romantic partner, no kids, and few friends, this was the stuff he lived for, the only thing he truly loved.

Digging into this man's mind, trying to pry clues from a brain that was, quite literally, atrophying, was probably the most fun he'd had in years.

And, if she was being honest, Claire enjoyed watching him do it.

Jack didn't think of himself as especially perceptive when it came to women, but even he could feel the heat in the car. He had driven them about an hour outside of Seattle to a town called Marysville, north of the city of Snohomish.

They'd spent the first half of the drive talking over the case, and Jack had complimented Kiko multiple times on her perceptive reading of the crime scene. He wasn't BS'ing her, either.

For someone as new as she was, with little experience at actual crime scene investigation, her reading had been impressive. He reiterated that he thought Claire was headed down the wrong path by focusing on Cunningham, but Kiko had been quick to point out that Claire had given Jack all the rope he needed. Maybe he would follow it and find something that broke the case wide open, or maybe he'd use it to hang himself.

"Either way," she had said. "I'm here for it."

During the second half of the trip, their banter had grown more overtly flirtatious. Jack had gone on a couple dates with Violet before knowing she worked for the FBI, but she'd made it clear that they had no future together the minute she learned that they'd be colleagues.

Kiko, however, didn't seem to care about those sorts of things, and had been flirtatious from day one.

After the intensity of the first case that had brought their small crew together, Jack had needed a couple of weeks to move into his new apartment. He'd told Kiko that he needed some time and space, but really he felt uncomfortable with the entire situation. Lately, she'd been pursuing him more aggressively, and, he had to admit, he didn't mind.

For the last few weeks, they'd been meeting up for coffee, dinner, and even a movie outside of work. They hadn't told Claire or anyone else, and Jack was worried that it was becoming obvious.

Despite being fairly aggressive at work, he'd never been that way with women. He was actually fairly shy. Kiko was not.

Now, as he turned onto a little side street, he felt the heat of Kiko's hand on his leg. He glanced over at her. "Not now. We really can't get into this now."

"As long as it doesn't affect our work," Kiko said, "we should do whatever we want."

"I'm afraid to find out what you *really* want," Jack said.

"You've been afraid of much worse, I think," Kiko said, her voice a feigned, ironically seductive tone that Jack actually found seductive, despite his efforts not to.

Thankfully, the GPS announced that the destination was ahead on the right, and Jack parked, shaking his leg gently, but enough to force Kiko's hand from it. "We need to lock in," he said, "both of us."

"No problem." Kiko's voice was back to normal, as though she'd stashed the other version of herself. She hopped out of the car and led the way up to the porch.

When Stacy Wegman answered the door, Jack noticed right away that she still looked like a badass FBI agent, despite being in her early seventies. She stood with her shoulders square, her grayish-blonde hair pulled back in a tight ponytail. She wore a black sweater with the sleeves pulled up around the elbows, revealing taut forearms.

Her eyes darted quickly from Kiko to Jack, then back to Kiko. "You're young," she said without introducing herself. "Both of you."

Jack extended a hand. "Jack Russo, and this is Vivian Greene. We call her Kiko. She may be young, but she knows what she's doing. As do I. We just want to talk a little bit."

Kiko shook Stacy's hand. "That's *Agent*, Kiko," she said, but the joke fell flat.

Stacy led them into an impeccably clean living room and pointed at a modest white sofa. "Yes, you said that on the phone, Agent Russo."

Jack cleared his throat as he sat. "As you know, we are looking into the case of the Interstate Reaper. Going through old case files, that sort of thing."

Stacy Wegman sat on the armrest of a recliner and watched him with an intensity that disconcerted him.

Jack felt like he was sitting for an exam. "Not that we are questioning *any* of the work you did back then, but we've been charged with looking into some old cases and this one came up. Still unsolved."

Stacy exhaled forcefully through her teeth, releasing air out of frustration. "Unsolved? I've known who the killer is for a few decades now."

"You have?" Kiko asked.

She nodded.

"Why were no arrests ever made?" Jack asked.

"Usual reason," Stacy said, standing and picking up a wooden baseball bat that had been leaning up against the wall. She took a slow practice swing, whooshing the bat through the air. "I keep this near the door. In case of intruders. Also because it helps me think better."

She'd been fairly intimidating *without* a deadly weapon, but now Jack pitied any intruder who made the mistake of picking her house to rob.

Pacing back and forth and passing the bat from hand to hand, she said, "Simon Santana Sanchez. Triple S." She shook her head, her face a mix of disgust and disappointment. "Bastard lives not an hour from here. Works at an auto junkyard in Sunday Lake."

"That's right on Interstate 5," Kiko pointed out.

"We looked at the file on him," Jack said. "Definitely lots of red flags."

She nodded. "Triple S is the Interstate Reaper. I have no doubt about it."

"If you're so sure, why was he just in the files along with the other four suspects? Why wasn't there more info on him? Unless we missed something..."

"You didn't," Stacy said, her voice tight. "Don't get me started on..."

"What?" Kiko asked.

Stacy sat again and rested the bat across her lap. "We had a thick file on him, and he was the guy. Eventually he made a deal to rat on someone in prison and he got himself officially cleared. The file disappeared." ·

Kiko looked at Jack. "Is that a thing?"

"Could be," he replied.

"No 'could be' about it," Stacy said. "We never had enough evidence to nab him, so eventually someone made a deal."

Jack glanced at Kiko, whose eyes were wide, then he locked eyes on Stacy. "Okay, so talk me through this like I'm twelve. How do you know he did it?"

Claire stood in the corner with her arms folded, watching Fitz go to work.

That day, Gus was dressed in dark blue pants and black shoes. Despite the room being fairly cool, he wore only a thin white T-shirt, almost an undershirt, as though he or someone who worked there had forgotten to get him fully dressed. But he didn't seem to mind.

When they'd walked in, he'd looked over at them immediately, as though he'd been expecting them, which Claire very much doubted.

Fitz shoved his hands in his somewhat wrinkled slacks and hovered over Cunningham. Apparently he didn't want to risk the plastic chair again. Fitz's size contrasted sharply with Cunningham's slight build, but he wasn't trying to intimidate him, at least Claire didn't think so. That worked in some kinds of interrogations, but this wasn't like anything either of them had ever been a part of.

"Where did you grow up?" Fitz asked.

When Cunningham didn't answer, Fitz leaned closer to him. "I already know the answer to that. Rural Louisiana, right?"

Still, Cunningham said nothing.

"Sometimes I think about my own old age," Fitz said. "I'd love to just stare out forever at a beautiful body of water. A lake, a stream, a river. Maybe even some wetlands."

Cunningham mumbled something.

Fitz leaned down. "What was that?"

Cunningham shook his head.

"There's just something about water that's peaceful," Fitz continued. He laughed to himself, a thick chuckle that Claire knew was somewhat forced. "Even after I die, I wouldn't mind staring out forever at a gorgeous piece of water."

Cunningham mumbled again, this time a little louder.

"What was that? Did you say *reserved*? Or was it deserved? Mr. Cunningham, Gus, you'll have to speak up."

Augustus Cunningham looked up at him, narrowing his eyes. "They all deserved it. All of them. For what *she* did. I wanted them to have to look at it forever."

PART 2

WALTZING THROUGH PURGATORY

CHAPTER THIRTEEN

INTERSTATE 5 STRETCHED out before them and Jack tuned the radio to a classic rock station. He'd always been fascinated with the seventies and eighties, even though those decades were well before his time. Something about the culture captivated him. The music, the clothes. Not to mention, those were the final decades of the pre-internet era. Jack himself had never known a time when he didn't have access to millions of people and unlimited information and entertainment via a simple internet connection. The folks who lived in the seventies, eighties, and into the nineties were the last ones who would ever know that world.

In his mind's eye, he saw it in sepia tone.

Kiko hadn't spoken in a while, and as he moved into the right lane to take the exit, he felt her eyes on him. She turned down the radio, which was playing Led Zeppelin, a band Jack knew well but, he feared, Kiko had never even heard of.

"Do you feel like you were born to do this?" she asked.

He glanced at her. "You mean be an FBI agent?"

She nodded.

"Something like that," he said. "When I was in the Special Forces, I felt like I was born to do that. This job is a little bit slower, but maybe I'm getting old."

Kiko laughed. "You're only six or seven years older than me. And I'm the youngest a person can be to get hired into the FBI. You're *not* old."

Jack took the exit, following the directions Stacy had given them. "Maybe I'm too old for you though."

"Bull. I read an article that tried to figure out what is a socially acceptable age gap between romantic partners. It said—well, of course, this is somewhat culturally dependent and whatnot—but they did their best to come up with a formula. You take the older person's age, divide it by two, and then add seven. You're thirty, right?"

Jack nodded.

"So, according to this article," Kiko said, "you would take your age of thirty, divide it by two, which is fifteen, and then add seven, which is twenty-two. That is the lowest age of a person you can date without it being creepy." She cleared her throat. "I just turned twenty-four."

"So, we're in the clear?" Jack asked.

"At least of the age thing. Though I don't think Claire would see it that way." She chuckled. "But I'm not planning to tell Claire a damn thing."

Kiko was quiet as Jack turned onto the little state highway that would take them a couple miles west to the junkyard.

"One thing I will say about Claire," Jack said, "is that she is perceptive. Strike that. *Very* perceptive. And she talks with Fitz, and you know Fitz has run psychological profiles on both of us."

Kiko laughed. "Life is too short to care about any of this. I mean, sure, there are rules and whatnot, and those rules are important, but you are not my boss and I am not your boss. There's no power imbalance here; there's nothing actually *wrong* with any of this, except in some HR manual somewhere." Her voice became more pleading, more sincere than he'd ever heard it. "There are a lot of things in this world that are *actually* wrong. Too many things. And this isn't one of them." She put her hand on Jack's shoulder. "Seriously, my mom died when I was a teenager. I never really knew my dad. In our job, you never know exactly how long you have. In this life, I do what I want."

Jack turned to her and smiled. "Good enough for me."

Mikey's Scrap Yard sat at the end of a long dirt road and was surrounded by an eight-foot-high fence with coils of barbed wire on top. A large entry gate had been propped open with a rusty gas can, and Jack drove straight in, stopping at a 12x12 shed that looked like it had been turned into an office of sorts.

Stacy's certainty about the guilt of the man she called 'Triple S' had been fairly convincing. He'd been an amateur photographer throughout the seventies and eighties and his trips had put him in the vicinity of at least three of the murders. And he had at least two accusations of assault against him that weren't in the files, both of women at rest areas along Interstate 5.

Stacy had investigated him for over five years and had interviewed him twice, but had never found enough evidence to convince a prosecutor. But for Stacy, the smoking gun was the fact that the murders stopped the same year Triple S was jailed for another offense. He'd robbed a jewelry store just outside of Seattle in 1990 and been convicted. Stacy's theory was that the years he'd done in prison had somehow broken him of the spell, which is why there hadn't been any new murders since he was released.

The first thing Jack heard when he opened the door was the sound of a barking dog and the rattling of a chain. Kiko, who had opened her door but hadn't yet gotten out, slammed it shut, trembling with fear.

Jack looked at her through the windshield. Kiko wasn't scared of much and could hold her own in almost any situation. But her fear of animals was almost comical. Jack also found it endearing.

Making sure Kiko could see him, he walked up to the dog, which appeared to be some kind of pitbull mix. He held out the back of his hand and the dog sat expectantly, stone still except for his tail which thwapped the ground emphatically. He calmed down as he sniffed, then enthusiastically licked Jack's hand.

Jack crouched and read the dog's name off his collar, which was in the shape of military dog tags. He turned and called to Kiko, "His name is Buster. Seems very friendly."

Slowly, carefully, Kiko got out of the car and walked in a half circle to stay as far away from Buster as she could, making her way through the open door of the little shed. The dog's tail went from vertical to horizontal wagging that repeatedly struck Jack's left leg as they both followed after Kiko. The dog stretched his chain as far as it would allow and Jack gave him a final pat on the head before following Kiko into the shed.

Seeing that there was no one at the counter, they walked through the back door into the dusty open-air junkyard. In a few spots, large canopies provided shelter for some of the cars that were being taken apart.

Jack heard clanging about fifty yards away and followed

the sound to where a stack of flattened cars sat next to a large truck with a man working under it.

"Excuse me," Jack called over the noise.

Slowly, a man who appeared to be in his late sixties, lying on his back and holding a wrench, scooched out from under the truck. He was bald and had multiple tattoos that had aged poorly, running up his neck and down his forearms. He was sweaty and dusty, and Jack was fairly sure this was Triple S. The man stood slowly, inspecting them as though they were unwelcome visitors, which they probably were.

"Jack Russo, FBI. This is Vivian Greene. By any chance, are you Simon Sanchez?"

The man squinted and used the back of his hand to wipe sweaty dust from his face. It made a muddy smear on his cheek and called attention to a tribal-looking tattoo below his left ear.

Suddenly, he pulled back his hand and threw the wrench directly at Jack's chest. It struck him hard and knocked him back. Gasping for air, Jack tumbled to the ground, and when he looked up, he saw the man sprinting across the lot.

Kiko was hot on his trail.

CHAPTER FOURTEEN

FITZ GLANCED BACK AT CLAIRE. She realized he was looking for approval and, she had to admit, she *did* approve. *They all deserved it. All of them. For what* she *did. I wanted them to have to look at it forever.*

What Cunningham had just said wasn't exactly an admission of guilt, but it was pretty damn close. She gave Fitz a nod as though he should continue, but before he could, there was a knock at the door.

Chris Thacker, the facility's executive director with whom she'd spoken the previous day, poked his head into the room. "Agent Anderson, may I speak with you for a moment?"

She wasn't certain she should leave Fitz alone in the room, but she did have more questions for Thacker. Joining him in the hall, but leaving the door open, she leaned on the wall a couple of feet from the room.

∾

"So, Gus," Fitz said, "tell me why they deserved it. What did they do that was so wrong?"

Cunningham didn't reply, and Fitz took a moment to watch his own mind as though observing it from the outside. As far as he could tell, it was barrelling down two parallel tracks.

One part had been disappointed when Claire left the room, especially accompanied by that tall drink of water nurse practitioner. He had to admit, during his questioning of Cunningham, he'd felt a bit like a little kid saying, "Mom, watch this!"

He wanted Claire to see how effective he was. This part he shoved to the back of his mind as forcefully as he could, like a pot of crummy leftover soup pushed to the back burner to steam away all day.

In the front of his mind, though, was a kind of freedom. Without Claire in the room, he could do things, say things, that he wouldn't if there were a witness present.

So when Cunningham didn't reply, Fitz scooched the little plastic chair forward, then put his elbows on his knees, which were nearly touching the old man's. He cradled his chin on his fists and leaned in, their faces now less than two feet apart. "Augustus Cunningham," he said, "we *know* about the murders. There were five of them. Bellingham. Portland. Seattle. Yreka. Grants Pass."

As he spoke the names of the cities, he watched Cunningham's eyes for any sign of recognition, but the old man's blank stare didn't change. Fitz saw no hint that Cunningham even registered the words he was saying.

"I *know* there are more dead women out there. I believe you started earlier, possibly in a different part of the country. And I know you can't always understand, don't know where you are half the time, don't know much of anything, but I also know that, somewhere inside you, there's a part that wants to admit it. A part that wants to tell me the truth. *Needs* to get it off your chest before you die."

Cunningham's eyes flicked toward Fitz, but he said nothing.

"Tell me about your mother," Fitz said. "Not your mother. I mean your aunt, the one who raised you." Violet had done a preliminary background check and learned that, when his parents died when he was a toddler, Cunningham had been raised by his single aunt in rural Louisiana. "Tell me, Gus, what did she do to you? Did she burn you with cigarettes? Hold your hand against the hot stove?"

His voice was becoming a deep hiss, not unlike the one Cunningham himself had unleashed once or twice. Fitz felt himself burning with an aggression, almost a rage, that he barely understood. Memories of his own mother were flooding through him, and he knew he was becoming angrier than he should, angrier than he had any right to be. During interviews, he sometimes used emotion to his benefit, but right now his anger was out of balance and wouldn't be useful.

He knew all this, but couldn't stop himself.

"Did she hold you over her knee and spank you for no reason? Or maybe she *had* a good reason? Maybe you were a bad little boy? Maybe you deserved *everything* she did to you."

The last words came out with a torrent of spit.

Cunningham's hands began to shake.

"Did you kill her?" Fitz demanded. "Was she the first? No, I bet you *ran* from her, I bet you were cowardly and moved across the country to get away from her. I bet you never even returned to your little hometown in Louisiana."

～

"Enjoying the weather?" Thacker asked. "It appears as though spring has sprung."

Claire, who wasn't really one for small talk, folded her arms. "That's what you wanted to talk to me about?"

He chuckled. "No, it's just that, I don't get a lot of chances to speak with other adults who don't work for me. Or aren't my patients. Sorry. I called you out here to let you know about a development in Mr. Cunningham's condition."

"Something you didn't tell me before?"

He frowned. "Not something we were *concealing*, but something that has come up more recently. You already heard about how he became somewhat aggressive with one of our staff members, Lydia. He has shown more signs of that in the last twenty-four hours. Not with Lydia as she is not assigned to him anymore. But he has lashed out verbally a couple times. Keep in mind, this is totally in line with his condition, almost to be expected really. In general, he is fairly low energy, almost sedated. But adrenaline can kick in, and he can become fairly combative."

"Violent?" Claire asked.

Thacker was slow to answer. "Hmmm, let me choose my words carefully."

Claire looked up at him, noticing that he was quite a bit taller than her, even though she herself was on the tall side. She put him at around six foot three and, though she wasn't good at reading the signs, she thought she was catching a slightly flirtatious energy from him. The attempt to talk about the weather, and now he was looking at her without answering, kind of cocking his head as though studying her face.

∾

Cunningham suddenly thrust his arms sideways as if he was swinging at something that wasn't there. Fitz lurched back instinctively, holding up his hands in defense.

But Cunningham didn't try to strike him. Closing his eyes, Cunningham tilted his head back and let out something like a growl, or possibly a howl, that seemed to be accompanied by a single word.

"Taaaaaayyyy-loooooorrrrrrrrrrr."

Taylor.

That's what it sounded like to Fitz, though it might have been "Tailor" or "Trailor."

Fitz was puzzling over this when the near-centenarian lurched forward. In one swift motion, with an unanticipated strength and violence, Cunningham pushed himself up out of his chair and crashed onto Fitz's lap.

Fitz yelped with pain as he felt Cunningham's teeth dig into the fleshy mass of skin where his shirt collar met the base of his neck.

Finally, Thacker said, "*Violence* implies intentionality. Sometimes two-year-olds throw tantrums when they don't get what they want, but you wouldn't necessarily call them violent, even though they might throw toys across the room. In the medical field we typically call these outbursts 'aggressive behaviors.' It's not really malicious; it's just a burst of energy, you know?"

"I see," Claire said.

"Before my wife passed away, she had a few bursts like that as well. So I know it on a personal level."

Thacker seemed fairly young for a man to be a widower.

"I'm sorry," Claire said.

He shook his head with a few short, quick bursts, like

he was erasing an etch-a-sketch. "No, *I'm* sorry. I shouldn't have brought that up."

"It's okay," Claire said. "If you don't mind..." she caught herself. Of course she wanted to know what happened, but it was entirely inappropriate to ask. Although he *had* brought it up.

"Melanoma is devastating," he said, reading her curiosity. "When her cancer metastasized to her brain, she developed dementia-like symptoms. She passed away three years ago." He bit his lip.

Claire could tell he was genuinely upset. "I really am sorry," she said.

Quickly, he gathered himself. "I apologize. I didn't have to bring that up." He shoved his hands in his pockets. "Well, I have to go finish a report, but I just wanted to update you on Mr. Cunningham's behaviors." He reached out and shook her hand, holding it just a beat longer than seemed normal, as he had previously. "Nice speaking with you again, Agent Anderson."

As Thacker retreated down the hallway, Claire heard a muffled shout from Cunningham's room and hurried back in, shocked to see Fitz struggling to push the old man off of him. And even more shocked to see that Cunningham appeared to be biting into Fitz's neck like a starving vampire.

CHAPTER FIFTEEN

KIKO COULD HAVE CAUGHT up with Sanchez almost immediately, but she held back, wanting to see where he was headed as she pursued him through the junkyard. The man was at least forty years older than her and, though spry for his age, he seemed to have a limp that protected an injured left foot.

He turned between a line of busted-up trucks, angled around a lone tree, and then took off at a full, hobbling sprint toward the pickup truck in the corner of the lot. That was when she decided to end the chase.

Picking up speed, she gained ground. Twenty yards from the truck, she launched, tackling him from behind and pressing his face into the dust. Kneeling on his back, she twisted his left arm behind him and held it in place. He offered little resistance. With her other hand, she twisted his right arm and then pressed both hands, one on top of the other, into his back while she pulled out a pair of zip ties. Applying them gracefully, she stood up and yanked him up along with her.

As she did, Jack skidded to a stop. He stood behind

them, breathing hard and holding up a hand to his chest, looking both impressed and a little bit embarrassed.

"I may be afraid of dogs and bulls," Kiko said, "and, well, anything that walks on four legs, but I'm not afraid of this bastard." For emphasis, she lifted up Sanchez's tied hands and he bent forward, then raised onto his tiptoes trying to keep the pressure off his scapula. He shifted in a sort of jive-style dance motion, trying to keep his bum foot from bearing too much weight.

Jack took him by the arm and began leading him in the direction of their SUV. "You and I are going to have a nice chat, Mr. Sanchez."

Sanchez spat on the ground. "All cops are pigs."

"Is that so?" Jack feigned surprise, "Well, I love pigs. They might get a bad rap, but they're truly lovely animals and more intelligent than people give them credit for."

Kiko led them towards the vehicle. She was happy to let Jack lead the way, as, despite her best efforts at pretending not to be, she was winded, and the adrenaline coursing through her veins had left her a little bit shaky. "Intelligent or not," she said. "I don't like pigs."

"She's afraid of them," Jack said to Sanchez.

"It's more nuanced than fear," Kiko corrected.

"Don't like dogs, don't like bulls, don't like pigs." Jack grimaced as he rubbed his chest where the wrench had struck. "Are there any animals you *do* like Kiko?"

"I used to like *you*, but I'm reconsidering my feelings." Kiko stopped abruptly when she heard clanging off to her right.

"What is it?" Jack asked.

"Take our guy to the SUV. I'll meet you there."

Walking towards the sound, Kiko saw two men. The older of the two was hitting a bumper with a rubber mallet while the other watched intently. The young one spotted

Kiko and tapped the other on the shoulder, causing him to set down the mallet.

They walked toward her, and immediately she could tell they were no threat. More than anything, they seemed surprised.

The younger of the two, who appeared to be around her own age, called something to her.

She couldn't make it out, but as she got closer, the older one seemed to repeat what the younger one had said. "What's going on?"

The younger one spat chewing tobacco onto the dusty ground as he stopped before her. "Always wondered when you folks would show up for that bastard." He let out a long, yellow-toothed laugh.

Kiko held up a badge. "Vivian Greene. FBI. We came to speak with Mr. Sanchez, and he attacked my partner."

The man with shaggy brown hair and a kind of diamond-in-the-rough handsomeness looked only a few years older than the tobacco-chewing man. "Your partner okay?" he asked.

"The bruises will heal faster than his heart when I break it," Kiko said.

"Awe snap. That's brutal," the younger man said. "Where's Sanchez now?"

"He's being detained." Kiko pointed a thumb in the direction where the SUV was parked.

"No skin off my nose," the younger one said.

"I need to take Sanchez off the clock," the other man said. "Never wanted to hire that guy in the first place, but they give us a check for it."

"What do you mean?" Kiko asked.

"Federal program. They help us pay the salary of former felons who are released. That guy could fix a truck like nobody's business, but I never trusted him and I never liked him."

"Tell me more," Kiko said. She leaned against a rusted car, her badge still prominent in her hand, her stance casual but her gaze sharp. "So, you've been paying him through a federal program? I take it that means you knew about his prison time?"

The man nodded. "Not a lot of applications for minimum wage with experience fixing trucks or scrapping them when they're beyond salvage."

"What else do you know about him?" Kiko felt herself laying on the warmth, which she knew he could misconstrue if she let him.

The man shifted uncomfortably, glancing at his companion. Kiko noticed the hesitation and smiled slightly, a disarming gesture to contrast with the directness of her questioning. "It's important," she added softly, "you could really help us out here."

The man rubbed his chin, eyeing Kiko as if measuring her sincerity. "Well, he *did* mention some messed-up stuff now and then," he admitted. "Talked about his childhood a bit. Said he used to mess with animals... not in a good way, you know?"

Kiko's face hardened just a touch, her eyes narrowing. "Messed with animals? Like, he hurt them?"

"As a kid, I guess," he said. "His father taught him *catch and don't release,* he called it. He told some story about taking down this mare that his father wasn't strong enough for. Bragged about it like I brag about leading the county in passing yards as a high school senior." The man blushed and looked at the ground. "That was a while ago now. I was a quarterback."

Kiko stowed her badge and put her hands on her hips. "You certainly look very athletic."

This brought a smile to the man's face.

"Did he ever talk about the women in his life?" Kiko pressed, stepping closer, her voice dropping to almost a whisper. This proximity, her assertive presence, seemed to unsettle the men even further.

"Yeah, he bragged about playing *catch and don't release* with women, too. Said they asked for it, gave consent and everything, only not all of them wanted to finish the game." The man looked down at his boots. "Never liked that talk. Made the crew uneasy, too."

"Thank you for telling me this," Kiko said. "It's helpful."

She could tell he'd already fallen for her. She had this effect on men from time to time. She wasn't above using it to her advantage when she needed to, but in this case, she hadn't meant to come on so strong. It was like she'd been pulled into playing the role she unconsciously knew he wanted her to play. She pulled out a business card and handed it to him. "If you think of anything else, call me."

"I... I will," he stammered, taking the card. "And maybe we could, I don't know... there's a drive-in movie theater."

"Are those still a thing?" she asked.

"They're making a comeback," he said hopefully.

Kiko switched back to business mode. "It's a work number. And you should only call it if you have more infor-mation about Mr. Sanchez, okay?"

The man looked up from the card and nodded.

She nodded back and offered a small, professional smile, then turned away to join Jack at the SUV.

CHAPTER SIXTEEN

CLAIRE EYED the sandwiches as Fitz set them out on the table in a neat row. "Which one is for me?" she asked.

"I ordered a bunch of everything, dearie. Buffalo chicken, a Reuben, a patty melt, a couple vegetarian things with cheese and roasted tomatoes. Or maybe hummus. Who can remember?"

Claire noticed that an extra-large sandwich had been pushed to the side, toward Fitz's seat. "And what did you get for yourself?" She pointed at the separated sandwich.

Each time they spoke, Ranger looked briefly into Fitz's then Claire's eyes before resuming his intensely focused stare on the food Fitz had been shifting about the table in front of him. Ranger's eyebrow movements showed his desperate—yet restrained—hope that he would be offered a morsel.

Fitz held up the giant sandwich. "This, my dear, is the Thanksgiving special. And, after getting bit by a possible serial killer, I think I deserve it. Thank you for intervening, by the way. In any case, this sandwich is the reason I order from Duke's. Double turkey, stuffing, cranberries, gravy, all on a quadruple size Parker House roll that they make special. Have a look at this side of warm gravy for dipping." Steam poured out of a little container as Fitz removed the lid.

Claire got a whiff of thyme and pepper. "A Thanksgiving special in April?"

"I nearly died when they took it off the menu in January. I told them I would boycott if they didn't offer it once a week as a special. And since I'm a key benefactor for their establishment, they obliged."

"Split it with me?" Claire asked.

"Not so fast. *This here...*" Fitz gently removed the sandwich foil as one might unwrap a cherished and delicate Christmas ornament, "...is the single greatest sandwich man has ever invented. I would be fine to get rid of Thanksgiving and all of its culinary trimmings, it's not my country's holiday anyway, but..." He made his voice an exaggerated southern drawl... "I would die fighting for America on account of this here sammich."

Puddles of drool formed below Ranger, who had stretched his vertebra to their limit as he craned his neck toward the sandwiches.

Fitz held his hand over his heart as though pledging allegiance to an unseen flag before picking up the sandwich and pointing it at Claire. "Get your own ruddy turkey sandwich, Claire Anderson. Despite my fondness for you, I will not be sharing a single Imperial inch."

"Fair enough." Claire shook her head as she watched him dip the sandwich into the tub of gravy before taking a bite so large that he barely had enough room in his mouth to allow him to chew. "You really are a piece of work, Fitzgerald."

Fitz winked at Claire. With his hands and mouth so full

of turkey sandwich, winking was one of the only gestures he was at liberty to use.

Violet, whom Claire had forgotten was even in the room, hit enter on her keyboard and the screen on the wall lit up. Claire recoiled slightly at the five faces.

"These are images of the five victims from within a year or two of their deaths. Took some digging and—"

Violet stopped abruptly when Kiko and Jack walked in.

"We've got Sanchez in the interrogation room," Jack announced loudly.

Fitz set down his sandwich and Claire braced herself for an eruption.

Jack had called on his way back and explained what happened with Agent Stacy Wegman and the apprehension of Triple S. He and Kiko believed they'd caught the Interstate Reaper. Fitz was fairly certain he'd coaxed a confession out of the Interstate Reaper back at the memory care center.

Whenever Jack and Fitz were in the same room, they tended to argue over anything they could. But now they had something definitive over which to disagree. Each believed he'd unmasked the Interstate Reaper, and they couldn't both be right.

"Here's how this is going to go," Claire said. "First, we are all going to eat sandwiches while Violet explains what she found. Next, we will see if we can get this Sanchez guy to talk." She held up a hand in Fitz's direction before he could swallow the bite he was chewing; she knew he was going to object and she wasn't going to hear it.

"I can stop you on that one," Jack said. "Sanchez has already lawyered up."

"Already?"

"He is a pro at this," Kiko said, sitting down next to

Jack. "Dude isn't especially articulate, but he knows the word 'lawyer' in half a dozen languages."

"Okay," Claire said, "so maybe we won't get anything out of him right now, but we can hold him for a day because of the assault on Jack. For now, let's all listen to Violet. Everybody grab your Thanksgivingless sandwich and dig in. You can't do good work on an empty stomach."

She waited as each of them selected a sandwich and noticed that, as Violet took one, she gave Kiko an odd look. Kiko, for her part, seemed as though she was trying not to acknowledge Violet's presence.

Claire filed this away internally. Something to deal with later.

Violet took her seat and unwrapped her sandwich, but before taking a bite, she launched into her presentation. "These are the five victims. Photographs taken in the year or two before they were murdered. I got some of them from newspaper clippings about their memorials. Some I got from family members I contacted. I ran some software over these images and, as you can probably tell, they all look somewhat similar. They're all white, all roughly the same age, all redheads. They all have facial features that indicate French and likely Irish heritage. There's no way," she continued, glancing at her sandwich with a half-smile, "that our perp ends up with this particular group of victims by accident."

"I'd add," Fitz said, "that I'd bet all of Jack's muscles that Cunningham's aunt who raised him, looked like these women."

"Can I just point out," Jack said, "that the original agent is certain *she* had the right guy. Sanchez has a history of abusing women. He drove up and down these routes. The murders stopped the moment he went to jail. I'm not as arrogant as Fitz; I won't claim that he is definitely our guy.

But we should at least respect the knowledge of our predecessors and look more into his past, right? If he won't talk, yet, let's at least check out his history."

Claire agreed. "Violet, get us everything you can about this Sanchez guy. We will keep trying to get information out of him, but I bet you can find more in an hour than we'll get out of him and his lawyer in a month."

"Will do," Violet said.

Fitz took another bite of his sandwich, then stood. He looked at Claire, asking for permission.

She nodded. "Go for it, Fitz."

"We visited Mr. Cunningham this morning," he began, "and I'm more certain than ever that he is our guy. I don't know about this Sanchez fellow, obviously not the kind of guy you want to bring home to your Mum. But it's Cunningham, I'm sure of it. I tried to provoke him today; that is, give a stir to the deranged killer still alive and well within him. In ninety percent of serial killer cases, once the killer is caught, it turns out there are victims that no one knew about. Victims that had not yet been connected to the known cases. I went in assuming this was the case, assuming that he had killed before. In my gut, I believed this could explain his initial move across the country. Perhaps he killed someone in Louisiana and moved west to get away from it. To get away from it and to convince himself that he could start again, be a different person, perhaps."

He glanced down at his sandwich as though contemplating another bite, then continued. "Anyway, when I got aggressive with him, he got aggressive with me." Fitz rubbed his neck. "He mostly got cloth, but he bit deep enough to break the skin before Claire yanked him off."

"Tell them what he yelled," Claire said, "and Violet, this is one of your next research tasks."

Fitz scratched his chin. "It was 'Taylor,' and I don't know if it was the name or the dude who sews suits. It could also have been 'trailer' or something like that."

"On it," Violet yelled through a mouthful of food. "I will run an analysis of every possible word that could have been and search it against our database of information for the guy. If this word has any relevance to his past, I will figure it out."

The intercom phone in the center of the table buzzed and Claire leaned forward to answer it. "Yes?"

"Claire, this is Cathy."

Claire knew that tone. "Lemme guess, Hightower heard about our little grand theft auto?"

"Hightower, and, well, you know who. But that's not all."

Claire sighed. "They want me up there?"

"I'll roll out the red carpet."

CHAPTER SEVENTEEN

CLAIRE LIKED HER DIRECT BOSS, Gerald Hightower. He had a straightforward way about him, and whenever she was meeting with him, she felt like they were on the same team. Jonathan Rivera—the esteemable J-River—not so much.

The door was open when she reached Hightower's office, but she could hear Jonathan's nasal voice wafting from it like a bad odor. "We simply can't have these sorts of violations," he was saying. "In all fairness, I expect you to put a stop to this."

Claire stopped in the doorway and Jonathan turned. "You mean put a stop to *me?*" Claire said, smiling with an overly sweet, sarcastic air.

Claire sat next to Jonathan, and now both of them faced Hightower, who folded his arms and leaned back in his chair.

Cocking his head toward Claire, Hightower said, "Tell me what happened with this car thing."

Claire felt like a kid at recess being questioned by a teacher over a case of a stolen peanut butter and jelly sandwich. It wasn't that she wasn't guilty, but there were certainly bigger issues that should have been pulling their attention.

She jabbed a thumb in Jonathan's direction. "This guy limited us to one car. We needed two. Jack and Kiko, I mean Agent Greene and Agent Russo, needed to head up north. They took the Escalade. Since I'm not supposed to use my personal vehicle, I borrowed one from the bureau."

"You *stole* a car," Jonathan said. "That vehicle was newly repaired and hadn't even passed all the inspections yet. When you brought the thing back, it was smoking. Now, the transmission is shot and that's going to cost another $3,000 in man-hours to repair. That should come out of your paycheck or, at the very least, your budget."

"Budget?" Claire asked. "What budget? I've seen lemonade stands at the end of a cul-de-sac with bigger budgets."

"Both of you, calm down," Hightower said.

Claire looked at him. "This guy has had it in for me since square one. I don't really know why."

Jonathan broke into a sarcastic tone, almost like he was speaking to a toddler. "I do not have it *in* for you, Agent Anderson. My job is to protect the FBI, not your little team of Avengers down in the Boiler Room. The *whole* FBI. Part of that is balancing many competing needs. A big part of that is the budget. I know that you think your cases are the most important thing the bureau has going on, but they are not."

"I don't think that," Claire said. "I think that our cases are important and that we should have chairs and a coffee maker and more than one car. At the very least, a car we can borrow from time to time."

"And *I think* that the men and women protecting Seattle's ports and airports from terrorists should have unlimited access to the cars they need when they need them as well. Go check the garage; are there infinite cars there?"

"No," Claire said, "but there are enough. You are messing with us because you believe in a strict hierarchy and that we are operating outside it. Just admit it. You don't want us to exist."

"That true?" Hightower asked.

He and Jonathan exchanged a long look, and finally, Jonathan let out a breath. "I'll admit that. I never denied it, in fact. And when you stole a car, you gave me enough demonstration of misconduct to make it so that you don't exist."

"Hold on," Hightower said. "Claire would probably admit that she should have gone through the correct systems. But that car was busted up anyway, and she's not paying for it. And it's certainly not a capital offense."

"It's her or me," Jonathan said softly. "And I think all of us know who the bureau needs more." With that, he spun on his heels, shoved his hands in his pockets, and walked out.

Claire, stunned at how things had escalated so quickly, shrugged in Hightower's general direction. "What the hell?"

"He's got a flair for the dramatic."

"I mean, would he really quit over this?"

"No," Hightower said. "But we need him. He's the lieu-tenant governor's brother-in-law. If Ridley trips over a banana peel, he's the *governor's* brother-in-law. Like it or not, we need this guy."

Claire shook her head. "More than you need me?"

"It's not going to come to that," Hightower said. "I'll smooth this thing over. In the meantime, Claire, please don't steal any more cars."

CHAPTER EIGHTEEN

BY SIX THE NEXT MORNING, Claire was back in the office and, for once, she had it all to herself. She had told everyone to arrive at 7 AM and had purposely come early. She knew this was going to be a hell of a day and she cherished the alone time in the office, drinking her coffee as the team filtered in.

She had planned to go over the crime scene photos again—this time in regular 2D—but she was distracted by a text that she couldn't get out of her mind. It had come the night before as she dropped Benny off at the home of her now ex-husband.

The divorce had been finalized only recently, and she had noticed a genuine change in Brian's behavior ever since. He was making much more of an effort with Benny. And not just buying him things or making grand promises. He was present. He showed up at Benny's swim event on time, even early. And he asked Claire if he could spend an extra week with Benny that month. He was taking time off work and was planning a whole host of adventures for them after school. Benny was thrilled, and he texted her late the night before saying they had been up playing video games.

As happy as Claire was that the divorce was final, she couldn't help but wonder where this surge of enthusiasm about parenting had been for the last twelve or thirteen years.

But it wasn't Benny's text that had her distracted. She had gotten a text from Chris Thacker that had kept her mind buzzing well past her bedtime and woken her up early. Now, glancing down at her phone, she read it again.

Claire, I apologize in advance as this is wholly unprofessional. But I wonder, would you be interested in having dinner with me? If this is out of line, just say so and I won't ask again. But, on your first visit, I did pull Agent Greene aside to ask her if there was any chance you were single. I couldn't help myself. If you'd like, we could keep it strictly about the case. But I know a great little Italian place only half a mile from your office. I'd love to take you out. Think about it?

The last thing Claire had been looking for when she went to Evergreen Memory Care was a date. But even she—busy as she was and as uninterested as she was in the dating scene—had felt a rush of excitement at the thought of the handsome nurse practitioner.

And the truth was, she didn't find his message especially inappropriate. Even though he was a relevant subject in this case, they weren't colleagues and never would be. He wasn't witness to a crime either, so it would not be an inappropriate relationship. And as far as the text went, although she was used to dating a couple of decades ago before there was such a thing as texting—or at least before she had a phone capable of it—she understood that this was how things were done now.

And as she tried to force her mind back onto the photos of the murdered women, she was considering his offer.

Making a split decision, she replied to his text.

Thanks for the invite. I'll think about it.

Just then, she heard Ranger's collar jangling down the hall. She knew that the heavy footsteps behind Ranger were Fitz's.

She flipped her phone over and looked up as Fitz entered.

He eyed her suspiciously. "You know, you have a terrible poker face, Claire. It's one of the things I appreciate about you."

Claire said nothing, just folded her arms. Then, just as quickly, she unfolded them because she needed another sip of her cappuccino. She had expected to have at least half an hour of alone time; Fitz had arrived early enough that she'd only had about ten minutes.

"Sometimes I wonder," Claire said, "whether God put you on this earth to annoy me."

"They do say that opposites attract, Agent Anderson."

Claire eyed him over the top of her cappuccino. Fitz had replaced his usual rumpled brown slacks and blazer with new blue ones. They weren't exactly clean or pressed, but they were clean*er* and *less* wrinkled.

He'd also recently claimed to have cut his drinking down to a few pints a day, which by body weight was probably equivalent to the one glass of red wine she drank in her little garden at the end of the day. His new appearance made her think of a scene from a movie in which a somewhat desperate and broken man had met the woman of his dreams in a coffee shop. His attraction to her had compelled him to purchase better clothes, begin working out, and generally clean up his act.

"Fitz," she said, "are you dating someone?"

He smiled ruefully. "Why do you ask?"

"Just, you seem different. I don't know."

"I'm holding out all my hope," Fitz said sarcastically, "that you will one day realize your undying love for me."

"Oh, please," she said.

Kiko jogged into the room and stood at the door, panting slightly.

"What's the rush?" Claire asked.

"I don't need a reason to run," she quipped. "I'm just enthusiastic about being alive."

Fitz shook his head. "I think we all know what, or rather *who*, you are enthusiastic about."

Claire swallowed hard. This was the last thing she wanted to get into.

Her phone dinged with a text and she flipped it over. It was another message from Thacker.

I just got into work and learned that my evening meetings were canceled. We could do dinner tonight if that would interest you.

Claire read the message twice before she realized that Kiko was standing behind her, reading over her shoulder.

Kiko grabbed her phone. "Has Agent Anderson found a love interest?" she quipped.

"Give me that," Claire said, standing and grabbing her phone back.

"The hot doctor?" Kiko asked. "You know, he asked about you. *Ooooohhhhh.* I had a feeling."

"Yes," Claire said, sitting back down and placing her phone on her lap. "He mentioned that he had asked about me."

"What are you two going on about?" Fitz asked.

"The doctor from the memory care facility," Kiko said.

"Oh, you mean the male nurse, who isn't a doctor *at all?*" Fitz asked.

"That one," Claire nodded. "He asked me out."

"Yum, yum," Kiko said. "That guy looks like a cross between George Clooney and Brad Pitt. Or McSteamy and McDreamy from *Gray's Anatomy*. If it didn't break the half-your-age plus seven rule, I would have asked him out myself."

"I wish I had half your assertiveness, Kiko." Claire was puzzled. "And wait, what is this age rule?"

"The socially acceptable age gap. Half the age of the older person, plus seven. So, like, a forty year old can date anyone twenty-seven or older. A sixty year old can date anyone thirty-seven or older."

"Bollocks," Fitz said. "Who came up with that useless drivel?"

"It's just like a social norm thing from a magazine I read."

"Okay, okay, I'm feeling the math," Claire said. "Things get a little wonky for people under the age of twenty two."

"Huh, I didn't think of that," Kiko said. "Anyway, the magazine wasn't for kids."

"So what did he say?" Fitz asked, turning to Claire. "The *nurse*."

Claire thought she detected a bit of irritation. "Just asked me out to dinner," she replied. "Nothing serious."

Fitz's gaze lingered on Claire with an intensity that belied his casual posture. He cleared his throat, the corners of his mouth twitching into a semblance of a smile. "He doesn't see you, you know? Not the actual real life blood and guts you, Claire."

"What's that supposed to mean?" Claire's voice was impatient.

"You're his *Beatrice*. He's just another infatuated Dante type, that's all I'm saying."

"Dante?" Claire asked. "What are you ranting about this time?"

"From *The Divine Comedy?*"

"I know what he wrote. What I don't know is what you're yapping about before I've even finished my first cappuccino."

"You may have three PHDs in psychology or whatever," Kiko said to Fitz, "but you're no great judge of character. How are those antibiotics working anyway? Is your neck bite healing?"

"It's just a flesh wound," Fitz answered.

Claire was growing frustrated and wasn't entirely sure why. "Say what you're going to say Fitz."

Fitz's voice dipped into the cadence of a lecture. "The story goes like this: Dante—the protagonist of *The Divine Comedy*—idealist that he was, had placed Beatrice, his love interest, on a pedestal, as though she were perfect. But he didn't actually *know* her in any real way. He projected the woman he created in his mind onto the Beatrice of the world." He paused as though waiting for a standing ovation.

Claire did not clap. "I'm familiar with the psychological concept of projection, Fitz."

Kiko groaned, "Give us a break Fitz, please." She stood and left the room.

"I'm with Kiko," Claire said. "But I *did* ask, so let's have the rest of your deconstruction of my as of yet non-existent relationship."

"I'm only saying," Fitz continued, undeterred, "he's met you twice, and only briefly. Now he wants to take you on a date?"

"That's how asking someone on a date works."

"Maybe, or it could be a poignant reflection on the nature of idealization, couldn't it? Your beefcake nurse could be projecting an idealized Claire onto the *real* you." He offered Claire a gentle, if somewhat rueful, smile. "This guy already thinks he's got your number. And he's wrong.

Don't you want to be with someone who at least knows they *don't* know the actual you? I think you might prefer to be *discovered*, Claire. Just a thought from your friendly local scholar of the human psyche."

Claire was about to launch a rebuttal when Fitz abruptly turned his attention to feeding a series of treats to Ranger, who had been wandering around the room checking the floor for food. The silence in the room felt a bit heavy, but Claire got a text that made her heart light up and took the weight from her shoulders.

This one was from Benny.

Dad just woke me up to get ready for school. Made me my favorite banana and peanut butter smoothie.

He added a smiley face emoji, and that was enough to bring a smile to Claire's face as well.

Soon after, Violet dragged herself into the room, Jack following a few minutes later. Now they all sat sipping coffees and chewing on bagels and muffins.

Kiko peered into the room from the open doorway.

"Come on in Kiko," Claire called out. "Fitz has left the lectern."

"Did he teach you anything of value?" Kiko asked.

"Only that I'd rather be trapped in a classroom with a bear than have Fitz deconstruct any of my relationships."

"Makes sense," Kiko said.

"She'll thank me later." Fitz nodded over at Claire who rolled her eyes. "You'll see."

Claire started the meeting. "Today is the day we solve this thing."

"And I have some good news on that front," Jack said. "I ran into Triple S's lawyer in the hall. He was meeting with his client and says that Sanchez is ready to talk."

"Talk about what?" Fitz asked. "He's innocent, at least of the crime we're investigating."

Jack ignored him. "Claire, do I have your permission to meet with them?"

Claire nodded. "Absolutely."

CHAPTER NINETEEN

MY MOTHER HAD BEEN HURTING me for years, but the first time I fought back was the same day I saw *How the West Was Won* for the first time. That morning she'd whipped me with her belt for no reason, or just because the anger came upon her, because I was being a *nuisance*, as she liked to say.

I still don't know *why* she did what she did.

All I know was that it hurt.

After the whipping I spent the day in the woods, throwing rocks at squirrels and rabbits. When noon hit I walked into town and used my last dollar—the dollar I was supposed to spend on chicken livers for dinner—to see John Wayne.

I'd always loved the grand scale and epic spirit of the American frontier, and *How the West Was Won* stole me away. I forgot all about the chicken livers.

The sweeping scenes and adventurous tales reminded me of the stories I'd read about the old days, filling me with nostalgia and pride for the pioneering spirit that had shaped America.

And it also filled me with anger, rebelliousness, and a desire to fight back.

When I got home and admitted that I hadn't got the chicken livers, my mother looked at me as though I was a cold-blooded killer.

"You what?" she asked.

She twirled a piece of her dark red hair around her index finger, then gave it a sudden tug, grimacing against the self-inflicted pain. She put the hair in her mouth and started chewing on it.

I folded my arms. "I saw the new John Wayne film instead."

Over the years, she used belts and switches and an old leather strap that her grandfather supposedly used on his horses. One time, when the anger had hit her, she'd even beaten me on the ass with a Bible.

That one had always struck me as particularly evil and contradictory. She was always more *spare the rod, spoil the child* than she was *turn the other cheek*. And that day she wanted to make sure that my stealing money to take myself to the pictures would be the last cheek of hers I'd ever slap.

But I was ready.

She darted around the kitchen table, trying to grab me, but I was quicker than her and dodged, using the table as a shield.

She grabbed a glass from the sink and threw it at me, but it hit my shoulder and shattered on the floor, doing little damage. I was still wearing my shoes, and she was barefoot, so when she came after me she got glass in her foot, which just enraged her more.

"I'll leave," I shouted.

I was thirteen years old, and I truly believed I could make it on my own.

"And go *where?*" she shouted back, her hair a tangled mess, her eyes full of fire.

"I'll go—"

I didn't know where I would go. I had few friends, no relatives, no safe space.

And that's when she knew she had me. "You'll go nowhere," she hissed.

I let her chase me through the house for another ten minutes before giving up. Better to take the punishment now than to wait until she got drunk and I fell asleep.

That day, she beat me to within an inch of my life, at least that's how I remember it. I didn't cry, though. Usually I cried but that night, something in me changed, and I vowed to get even.

As I went to sleep, bruised and bloodied, I thought about John Wayne and how he would handle this.

One way or another, I was going to get my revenge.

CHAPTER TWENTY

"PLEASE, CLAIRE," Fitz said, his voice genuinely pleading. "Don't let this bag of muscles and libido conduct an interview with a suspect."

Jack retorted, "I thought you said he wasn't a suspect because you're sure you already have the guy."

Fitz was flustered. "He *isn't* a suspect in *this* case, but he is well—something. One way or another, I should be the one to interview him."

Claire stood up, but before she could render a verdict, Jack kept pressing his case. "I found this guy. Kiko caught him, and we brought him in together. If you're so sure you have the right guy, Fitz, head down and get a confession; we can close this case. Meanwhile, if it's alright with you, Claire, I will see what I can get out of Sanchez."

Claire considered this. "Jack, you conduct the interview. Fitz, you need someone to go with you to the memory care facility." She glanced at Kiko.

Kiko said, "I helped bring Sanchez in. I want to be there for the interview."

Claire needed to stay behind to deal with a stack of

paperwork Hightower had sent down. Apparently, it was the only thing that would keep Rationing Rivera out of her hair for a while. "Violet, can you go with Fitz?"

"That's a good idea," Kiko said. She turned to Violet. "If you need anything from your computers, you can call and I will—"

Violet turned, her eyes wide. "Do. Not. Touch. My. Computers."

Claire had never heard such a definitive tone from her.

"Don't talk to me that way," Kiko said.

Violet was staring daggers at Kiko, and a pit formed in Claire's stomach. The last thing she needed was an interpersonal squabble, the nature of which was not entirely clear to her.

"Oh, now this is getting messy." Fitz was smiling broadly. He was almost giddy. He loved conflict for conflict's sake, at least when it didn't involve himself.

"Ladies," Jack said, trying to sound conciliatory, "I'm sure that Kiko won't need to use the computers, and Violet, even if she did, she's fully capable of looking something up on the Internet."

"She can use her phone," Violet snapped, clearly upset. "My setup is a sophisticated multi-server unit that runs on a proprietary software configuration. I've got algorithms running on this system that aren't available publicly, and it's set up to handle thousands of gigabytes of data. My system would find running a basic internet search *offensive*; I use it to develop and run high tech virtual reality replications like the crime scene simulation we used yesterday. It's delicate, customized, and critical to our operations. It's not something *Kiko* could understand."

The two stared each other down, and Claire knew she'd lost control of the situation.

"Kiko," she said, "you go with Jack and report back on

the interview with Sanchez. Violet, go with Fitz. I'll stay here. And don't worry, no one will touch your computers. We will address what is going on with your attitudes later."

Her tone did not offer any space for questions or replies, and Claire recoiled at the sound of her voice, which reminded her of how she sounded when her twin daughters would bicker endlessly during their adolescence.

One by one, the four of them filtered out of the room.

Ranger, sensing that she was the only one around who could be of any value to him, shuffled over and lay at Claire's feet. She put her hand on his head and scratched him behind the ears. He pressed into her hand, and Claire recognized this as his gesture to indicate that he liked whatever she was doing. The pit that had formed in her stomach had subsided a little bit, but had been replaced by a general uneasiness that filled her whole body.

Her phone dinged with another text from Thacker.

I don't know what it is about you, you are just captivating, something even beyond captivating. I know this probably is too forward, but I sense a deep connection between us, almost like it was meant to be. I hope you will consider my dinner offer tonight. They have an amazing wine list. How do you feel about Amarone?

The uneasiness in Claire intensified.

Two texts in under an hour, one of which was something damn near a declaration of love. Was this what they call *love bombing*? Or was it just normal dating etiquette? She had been out of the game for too long to know for sure, and she didn't have time to think about that now.

Kiko and Violet had seemed as though they might come to blows, and that was enough to destroy her task force if she let it spiral out of control. She needed to get to the bottom of whatever was going on. If it was as simple as jealousy over Jack, that could be addressed.

But she feared it was something more.

CHAPTER TWENTY-ONE

JACK RESPECTED FITZ. There was no denying that he was a brilliant interrogator in certain circumstances. But Jack was also confident that Simon Sanchez wasn't the kind of guy whom Fitz could easily crack. He was a hardened criminal who had done many years in prison. He was also no fool, as Jack could tell by the slight smirk on his face as he entered the interrogation room with Kiko.

He had the look of someone who was in on a joke that Jack had been left out of. That was fine. Because Jack was standing there with his arms crossed, a free man, while Sanchez had been handcuffed to the table. Next to him, a muscular young lawyer sat with his too-small hands folded politely in front of him. His eyes were hard, and he looked like the type who wouldn't take any crap from anyone.

"I'm not going to mess around," Jack said, "we already have you for assaulting a federal agent. With your record, that's enough to put you in for the rest of your life." He let that hang in the air as he pulled out a chair for Kiko, who sat, and then one for himself. Jack took the seat across the wide table and stared at Sanchez. "I know you may not enjoy your job," Jack said, "but I doubt you enjoy prison food either."

"I'm not going back to prison." Sanchez scratched at a tattoo on his neck.

Jack couldn't see it clearly, but it looked to be a typical skull and crossbones thing, the kind he'd seen a hundred times on a hundred crooks.

"Tell me a little bit about the women you assaulted," Jack said.

Sanchez shrugged. "Hey man, it was all purely consensual. They asked for it and they had it coming."

The lawyer tapped on the table with a pen. "My client isn't here to speak about past alleged crimes for which he was unjustly incarcerated, and he's *definitely* not here to talk about alleged assaults for which no charges were ever filed." He cleared his throat. "We understand that you are dredging up old cases in which he was never formally accused of anything. The Interstate Reaper killings. We will answer questions on that subject."

Kiko rapped her knuckles on the table. "Just because he was never arrested doesn't mean there isn't a mountain of evidence that shows he's the Interstate Reaper."

"Those women probably had it coming, too," Sanchez said.

Kiko pushed back her chair like she was going to stand, but Jack held her back. He could tell that Sanchez was about to launch into something, and he wanted to hear him out.

"Most women have it coming." He puckered his lips and looked at Kiko. "You're probably asking for it from somewhere. Got some things coming, too, I'd imagine."

"You'd do well to keep me out of your imagination," Kiko said, her lips tight.

Jack could feel her arms shaking as she spoke.

Sanchez grinned, revealing a single gold tooth on the top row. "The way those ladies got to stare out at the water after they were gone... Hell, at least they had a nice view."

Jack swallowed hard. He leveled his eyes on Sanchez. "What did you say?"

"Spoiled *nuisances* like them feel entitled to a nice view. They'd be expecting to be left looking out at the water for the rest of eternity."

"How did you know they were left staring at the water?" Kiko asked.

Jack had been poised to ask the same thing. As far as he knew, that piece of evidence had only been discovered while Claire was inside Violet's 3D crime scene rendering. Of course, the locations of the victims had all been covered by the press when the bodies were found, but not the positioning of the bodies.

Sanchez shrugged.

Jack narrowed his eyes on Sanchez, who narrowed his eyes right back.

It was a staring contest, and Jack didn't intend to lose.

CHAPTER TWENTY-TWO

"FOR THE LIFE OF ME," Fitz said, "You drive like you learned to drive playing video games."

Violet slammed on the breaks then, just as abruptly, hit the gas and swerved around a bus.

Since Jack and Kiko were back at the office, Fitz had been able to sign out the Escalade, though Violet had insisted on driving to Evergreen. Letting her drive was his first mistake of the day, but it wouldn't be his last.

She took the corner into the parking lot too sharply and at too high a speed, struck the curb, then veered into a parking spot before slamming on the brakes only inches from another car. She turned to Fitz. "I never really *learned* to drive, strictly speaking."

Fitz shook his head. "Please don't tell me—"

"I hacked into the system and faked my driving test, which allowed me to *re-order* my driver's license even though it was actually my first."

Fitz sighed. "So, essentially, you committed a Washington state felony?"

"Technically, I did it while I was seventeen and still in

Massachusetts. So, I'm not really sure I could do any time for it now. Statute of limitations, or whatever."

"Does that make it any better?" Fitz asked.

"Does it make you feel any better about letting me drive?" she countered.

"The fact that you are a federal law enforcement agent makes me fear for the future of this country." Fitz let that hang in the air and got out of the car.

Violet followed him and they made their way to the memory care unit.

"I'll make you a deal," Fitz said. "I won't tell Claire what you just told me if you don't tell her about the tactics I'm going to use in there. I have a feeling this interview is going to go terribly awry. And yet, today is a day I make all the mistakes."

"Why would you *want* to make mistakes?"

Fitz shrugged. The truth was, he didn't know. But sometimes the desire to screw things up became too strong to ignore.

After signing in, Fitz headed to the little sitting area, where he had conversed with Sister Ella a few days earlier. He was hoping she was there again, and she was. Leaning forward and resting his hand on the table, which was bare save for her empty coffee cup, Fitz said, "Hello, ma'am. Might we sit down for a moment?"

She didn't look up, didn't speak.

From behind, a nurse Fitz didn't recognize said, "She hasn't been speaking much today. At least not in English."

"What has she been saying in Italian?" Fitz asked.

The nurse put her hands on her hips. "Would you like me to find the landline and get our third party agency translator on the phone? I can do that for you, but it will be another hour before I can. I won't finish passing medications to the rest of the patients any sooner."

Fitz shook his head and the nurse returned to her cart.

"*Salve signora.*" Fitz tried to catch her attention, but the old woman's eyes were locked on the coffee cup. That was all the Italian he knew besides various quotes from literature he'd put to memory to impress others. Besides, he likely botched the pronunciation such that she might not recognize he was speaking Italian in the first place.

Violet held her phone in front of Fitz's face. "This might help."

"What is it?" Fitz asked.

"Almost instant translation," Violet explained. "Just speak into the phone."

Fitz cocked his head, impressed. Then he thought for a moment and said, "Hello, ma'am, I wanted to ask you a question about what you said about Mr. Cunningham a few days ago." He paused, and only half a second later a confident-sounding male Italian voice emerged from the phone, repeating his question.

The woman didn't look up, but he saw a flicker in her eyes when she heard her first language. Then Violet moved the phone back in front of Fitz's lips. "You said that he was a very bad man. What bad thing has he done? If you do not feel safe, we can help you."

Violet held the phone in front of the woman and again she listened, this time showing more interest.

"Please," Fitz said into the phone when Violet moved it back in front of his lips. "Please help us. What do you know?"

The woman looked at the phone suddenly, as if jolted awake. She spoke softly, her voice a hoarse whisper, and in an Italian accent so thick, Fitz felt transported to a time long ago.

Per quanto riguarda come sapessi che fosse cattivo, ci sono cose che semplicemente sappiamo nel cuore....

She kept speaking, but Fitz tuned her out. He couldn't understand the words anyway. Instead he focused on her face, which had become clear and bright as though she'd suddenly remembered who she was, where she was, and what her life was all about.

Fitz waited for her to finish, then listened closely as Violet moved the phone up to his ear. The voice that came through the phone was deeply incongruous as it was much younger than the woman and sounded upbeat and positive, a stark contrast to the words. "As for how I knew he was bad, there are some things we just know in our hearts. There is no explaining it. But two days ago, two days ago, I was sitting by the window staring out at the little pond off the breakfast room. Mr. Cunningham rolled his wheelchair up beside me. I could feel his icy stare. I could feel his anger. Feel his terror. And he said to me, 'If I was still strong, I would make you stare at that little pond forever, you little nuisance.'"

Fitz looked over at Violet. "Is that thing recording?"

"Automatically."

"Claire wanted a smoking gun, as if we needed another. I think we have it, and I think I can get us more."

As Fitz entered Cunningham's room, he had the strange sensation that this was the last time he'd see the man. They already had enough to arrest him, although Fitz didn't believe Cunningham would ever go to trial or pay for his crimes. Cunningham would likely be dead within a year or two, and no judge on earth would throw him in jail. Perhaps he would be placed in a more restrictive facility, at least that would save people like Lydia and Sister Ella from more abuse. But even that was not guaranteed.

At this point, Fitz had to admit that Jack had been right —he wanted to prove Cunningham was guilty just because. Sure, it might also bring some satisfaction to the families of the victims. It would close a case and look good on their record. But in his heart of hearts, Fitz knew he was a selfish bastard. He just wanted to win, and as he sat in front of Cunningham for what he believed was the last time, he intended to do just that.

Violet had posted herself up against the wall, arms folded and looking as disinterested as ever. Cunningham sat as usual with his hands folded on his Afghan, staring out the window as a breeze ruffled the needles of a small pine tree.

"Taylor," Fitz began, "tell me about Taylor."

Violet had searched every record she had and found no reference to a Taylor—either the name or the profession. She had tried 'trailer' and other variations, but nothing relevant had appeared.

Cunningham moved his head toward Fitz slowly, and his eyes showed a lucidity Fitz had never seen there before. But he didn't answer the question.

Instead, he began in a louder, more confident tone than Fitz had heard from him. "When I was little, I spent a lot of nights watching the water. The shadows were always watching me back."

"What water?" Fitz asked. "A lake, a river, an ocean?"

Cunningham shook his head. "She made me watch the water."

"Taylor?" Fitz asked. "Did Taylor make you watch the water?"

He shook his head. "*She* made me, and then I made her."

"Have you ever been to Bellingham, Washington?" Fitz asked.

Cunningham shook his head.

"What about the Rogue River outside of Grants Pass, Oregon?"

He shook his head again.

Fitz jabbed a meaty finger at him, stopping only an inch in front of his chest. "In 1983, you were in Portland, Oregon. Crystal Springs Lake. Is that a body of water you remember?"

Still, Cunningham said nothing. Simply shook his head.

"And in 1986, you were in Seattle. You had just opened a new Sunny Skillet Diner. You strangled Caroline Smith and left her in the wetlands. Do you remember *that* body of water?" Fitz's voice was growing heated, as though it could break Cunningham in half. "Yreka, California," Fitz continued. "Susan Swanson. That one was your mistake. That's where you got your voice recorded." Fitz made his voice a thin hiss. "You little *nuisance.*" He paused, watching the flicker in Cunningham's eyes. "Susan Swanson was a nuisance, right Gus? Just like the one who made you look at the water, just like Taylor probably. How many more women are there, you sick twisted bastard!"

Cunningham started shaking. "Taylor did nothing wrong. Taylor is an angel. I saved her. She was perfect. We forget nothing." He closed his eyes and began running his hands along his legs, as though soothing himself.

But then Fitz noticed that he wasn't running his hands along his legs. There was a strange shape under his Afghan, something square, like a vinyl record case or something. Fitz pulled off the Afghan and saw that he was running his hands over his photo book, the one he'd looked through during their first visit.

Fitz had already looked through the book and found nothing of interest. Mostly photos of Cunningham with coworkers out front of new Sunny Skillet diners up and down Interstate 5. There was nothing in there that went beyond what they already knew. But there was something in the way he was rubbing his hands over it. Something grotesque and sickening.

"Who is Taylor?" Fitz demanded. "Is she in this book?"

He didn't wait for a reply. Fitz grabbed the book and stood up, avoiding Cunningham's outstretched arms.

Cunningham tried to stand, but he was too weak. He flopped back in the chair.

Fitz nodded toward the door, indicating that Violet should stand in it to block anyone from coming in. He furiously thumbed through the photos, but still saw nothing of interest.

Then he felt it.

The back cover of the photo book was heavier than the front, despite being the same size and thickness. Examining it, he realized that photos had been hidden between the cover and the thick, cream-colored paper that was partially glued to the inside of the cover.

Fitz held up the book and smiled down at Cunningham. "Is Taylor in here?"

"No, no, no," Cunningham said. "Taylor's not there."

CHAPTER TWENTY-THREE

THE SMIRK on Sanchez's face had lasted long enough for Jack to reach his breaking point. There was no way Jack would jeopardize the case by getting physical, even though that's exactly what he wanted to do.

With Kiko there, not to mention the lawyer—who would just love to slap Jack with an assault charge of his own—he had to be more careful.

"Your smirk tells me you think you can get away with hinting at the truth, like OJ did with that stupid book 'If I Did It' and that stupid interview. That you can taunt us, whisper little details of the murders without admitting anything. But it doesn't matter because we are going to *prove* your guilt. Not to mention the fact that you're still going to be in jail for the rest of your life for assaulting me."

Sanchez let out a long, bellowing laugh that was totally incongruous with the rest of his speech and personality. "You think I'm smirking because I did it. No, I'm smirking because I *didn't* do it, and the evidence I have to prove it is going to keep me out of prison."

∼

Fitz wedged his finger between the back cover of the photo book and the thick paper, then pulled out the photographs. Still in his wheelchair, Cunningham stared off into space and started mumbling. "Not a nuisance at all....there we are...come one now, here kitty, kitty. Sweet Taylor." Then he started to sing, "*And I need you more than want you...*"

Fitz thumbed through the photos one by one. He recognized the landscapes, even some of the brambles and brush. But the angles on the bodies were different from what he had seen on the screen of Violet's 3D rendering.

These were not professional crime scene photographs. They were amateur black and whites. Most likely, someone had developed them in some sort of private darkroom. Most likely, that someone was Cunningham himself, although Fitz's mind was unable to forget the fact that Sanchez had been an amateur photographer.

Fitz thumbed through them once, then one more time, then handed them to Violet.

Her voice didn't sound surprised as she thumbed through them and said each woman's name aloud: "Sandra Ireland. Francis Graber. Pamela Crane. Caroline Smith. Susan Swanson."

"No Taylor," Fitz said.

"No Taylor," Violet echoed.

She handed the photographs back to Fitz, who sat back down in front of Cunningham. The evidence was now absolutely insurmountable. The case was closed.

Still, Fitz wanted to hear him say it. "You killed these women," he stated, his tone neutral.

Cunningham said nothing.

"Are there more than these five?"

Still, Cunningham said nothing.

"Who is Taylor?" Fitz asked.

Cunningham shook his head.

Fitz glanced up at Violet, who shrugged.

"We've got this old bastard dead to rights," she said. She nodded towards the door. "Let's just go before the guy bites you again."

Jack felt his fists clench under the table and tried to remember what he'd learned on a calming app he'd downloaded the day before. It had given him tips on how to relax in stressful moments, but he couldn't remember the breath pattern it had taught him. He unclenched his fists, took in three deep breaths for good measure, then turned to Sanchez's lawyer.

"Here's the deal," Jack said. "If the next sentences out of your client's mouth aren't a detailed and straightforward explanation about everything he knows regarding this case, giving us the whys and hows of the guilty, we're walking out of this room and filing charges. We have a witness from the scrap yard who saw the assault, not to mention Special Agent Greene, who has an exemplary record, who can also testify. Your client will be in jail for the rest of his life starting by the end of today unless the next things I hear are clear and actionable statements." He pressed his hands into the table and gave an unwavering stare at the lawyer.

The lawyer stared back, but his eyes were shifty and Jack knew he'd gained leverage. The lawyer leaned over to Sanchez and whispered something in his ear. Sanchez shrugged as though this was exactly what he'd expected to happen.

"So I robbed a jewelry store, and they caught me for it. I

served my time, buddy. They say I beat up some women, and maybe I did or maybe I didn't, but no charges ever came of it. Never killed no one, though. Would have liked to a few times, but who wants to do that kind of time? Eight years I did in Clallam Bay. Another two at Coyote Ridge. In between, I had a nice stay at WSP for six months. Became friends with a real sinister bastard there, Jake Whitehall." Sanchez paused, watching Jack's face.

Jack had felt his expression shift, revealing that he'd recognized the name. Times like this he wished he could be more like Kiko, able to shapeshift in such a way that the people around her only believed what she wanted them to believe. He knew that she even used that kind of power on him from time to time. She was like some kind of emotional chameleon with the power to bewitch. He, on the other hand, wore his emotions on his face.

Whitehall was a notorious serial murderer who'd killed four members of his family before going on a nine-month rampage across Washington State. He tortured and killed six young men whom he met in bars and clubs. When he'd finally been caught, they found severed limbs and heads of some of the men in a large chest freezer in Whitehall's basement. It sickened Jack just to hear the man's name.

"Whitehall makes me look like a choir boy," Sanchez said, "and I think you know that to be true. Anyway, he was obsessed with himself and his own press. Obsessed with others like him. Ted Bundy. The Green River Killer. That Zodiac thing in New York or wherever. And he was obsessed with the Interstate Reaper, too. Read everything about that killer. Knew everything about the case. He even traded an exclusive jailhouse interview with some newspaper for inside scoops that never went to print, like the idea that the women were all facing the water for their eternal sleep. He said he was just interested, but I think he was jealous that whoever that guy was, he was still free, still capable of killing. He knew he was never getting out of prison, so he had his lawyer sneak newspaper clippings inside the legal documents during their meetings. That lawyer was a sick bastard—I guess he felt he owed Whitehall for the free publicity representing the infamous Whitehall had given him. He even bought and brought him a tube of that Garnet Devotion he'd been begging for."

Jack froze. Before hearing the words 'Garnet Devotion,' he had fallen into a daze in the same way he did when his grandmother told him stories of his Native American ancestors, or his nonna explained in excruciating detail how to make their family's ancestral risotto recipe.

Sanchez's story about Whitehall was similarly conveyed. Like it was legend.

But the mention of Garnet Devotion lipstick changed everything. He'd read in a police report that hikers had found a tube of it about ten yards from the site where Caroline Smith's body had been found. This evidence had appeared in only one police report, and there was little chance any reporter had gotten wind of it.

So there was no way Whitehall could have known about it, even if he *had* researched every piece of the case while in prison. That meant there was no way Sanchez could know about it either.

Kiko seemed to be on the same page. "The lipstick," she said.

"That's the kind of detail we're looking for," Jack said. He turned to the lawyer. "But how is it that your client knows information about this murder that was never revealed in the press?"

Sanchez frowned. "Look, I don't know *how* Whitehall knew about the lipstick. But the guy told me every detail of the case. Guess he figured I was interested since I told him

I had been a suspect before I got banged up for the jewelry store thing. And he knew I hadn't done it, too. Whitehall was a great deal smarter than the lot of you pigs. That's for sure." Sanchez shook his head. "It's Whitehall's damn stories. That's how I know what I know."

CHAPTER TWENTY-FOUR

CLAIRE DROPPED the paperwork on Kathy's desk and frowned. "That ought to keep Jonathan busy for a while."

Kathy smirked. "My thought is, with all the paperwork created by his BS, he's going to have to hire himself an assistant to process it. But *he's* the one who would have to approve the expense for his own assistant, which he'd never approve, thereby creating a never-ending doom loop in which he must have and can't get the help he needs."

"Just desserts." Claire laughed. "I'd enjoy that a little too much. Seriously though, Kathy, if there's anything you can think of that will help to keep Hightower off our butts for a little while, it would be appreciated."

"I'll try bringing him decaf for the next few mornings and see if he notices. You just keep filling out that paperwork ad infinitum until I need to work overtime to process it. Maybe my bloated paycheck will scare him into finding you a car, or maybe I'll make enough overtime money to buy that second car for your team myself."

"Thanks, Kathy. If you do land that overtime paycheck, promise me you'll find something more fun to spend the extra money on." Claire tapped the desk and headed out.

She decided to take the stairs down to the Boiler Room. Even steps downstairs counted as steps on her personal health app. When she'd decided to retire, she'd slowly lost a tiny bit of her fairly athletic build. Having that extra half glass of wine here and there or making her daily walk a mile instead of two had slowly changed things. And ever since the sprint from her house across the beach toward the ferry in pursuit of the Luminist killer, Claire had been trying to get back into better shape. Avoiding the elevator was part of her plan.

She was still fairly fit, but if she was going to lead this team, she felt she owed it to them to be at her best, both physically and mentally. Sometimes she counted the steps, creating a kind of internal tracker to see how accurate she was. At various points throughout the day, she would compare her mental tally to the tracker in her watch. Stopping at the base of the stairs, she checked her watch, figuring she must be around 5,000 by now. She was disappointed to see that she was only at 3,100 steps for the day. Maybe she could pace during the meeting.

As she reached the door, she realized the meeting was already in full swing, and there was a heated argument under way. But for once it wasn't Jack and Fitz going at it.

"I didn't touch your computer," Kiko was saying.

"I left it running," Violet declared. "When I got back, it was turned off."

"Maybe the power flicked off or something. Or maybe you were too distracted by whatever new Marvel movie came out last night or whatever." Kiko was throwing insults from the hip.

Violet scoffed. "You think I don't know what state of function my computers are in when I leave a room? I've been turning computers off and on since I was less than two years old."

"I don't really care what you think you know," Kiko shot back. "Why the hell would I touch your stupid computers in the first place?"

"Stupid?" Violet asked, incredulous. "These computers are a thousand times smarter than you. And unlike some, they have respect for rules and actually *follow* them."

"You, of all people, want to toss shade on a person for rule breaking? Ms. Expelled-from-MIT-for-Stealing-Bitcoin."

"I didn't steal bitcoin," Violet corrected. "I stole computing power to *mine* bitcoin."

Kiko scoffed again, then noticed that Claire had walked in and lowered her voice. "I don't know. Can't you just ask the computers who turned them off or something?"

"Ladies," Claire said. She held back her instinct to say *knock it off*—or something equally motherly, then opted for a more generic, "Let's work."

Kiko stepped back, seemingly unbothered by the interaction. She took a seat next to Fitz, who had a self-satisfied grin on his face.

Before Claire could ask for his report, Fitz said, "Well team, as I said before, we've found our killer. Violet, can you throw the photographs up on the big screen?"

His usual egotistical tone was more subdued, and Claire understood why. At times Fitz used his arrogance to mask uncertainty. But this time he wasn't uncertain. He'd been right the entire time, and now he had the proof.

Fitz said the names of the five women as Violet clicked through their photographs. "These images were directly under our noses, in Cunningham's possession the whole time. Mementos. All five of the victims are pictured *after* they were killed but *before* their bodies had been found. *Not* from newspapers, *not* from the public record, not even from police files. If there was any doubt before, which there shouldn't have been, there isn't now. Gus is our killer."

He folded his arms and looked at Jack. "Anyone care to object? No? You there, the buff lad in the corner, you have anything to add?"

Apparently when it came to Jack, Claire thought, Fitz could be both certain and arrogant.

Jack shook his head. "I guess it's over. We thought we had something with Sanchez, and I'll want to interview him again, but when Fitz is right, he's right."

Claire thought she saw Kiko flash a questioning look towards Jack. "You have thoughts, Kiko?" she asked her.

Kiko shook her head.

"Okay then. But Jack's wrong," Claire said. "There will be paperwork. This case is far from over. Fitz, did you—"

"I called Hightower, and he called in a favor to get an officer stationed outside Cunningham's door. Now that we know for sure it was him, we owe it to the staff of the facility to do at least that. I still don't think he poses any actual threat."

"So long as you don't let him get too close to your neck," Jack said.

"Right," Fitz agreed. "But I'm no red headed young woman alone in the woods with the guy. That bite was the dementia talking."

Claire said, "I don't know why I don't feel better, but we should all feel good about this. Jack, you did the due diligence and we can officially clear Sanchez."

"Right," Jack said. "I'll give Agent Wegman a call and tell her what happened. She worked hard on this and she deserves to know."

"Good," Claire continued. "Kiko, I think you should call Lydia at the memory care facility. She put us onto this guy and she was right. Implore her not to talk about this publicly. I think we can trust her."

Kiko looked over at Jack, then said, "I can do that."

"Violet, if you could start putting together a report, I'd appreciate it." Claire sat and allowed Ranger to place his head on her lap and rubbed behind his ears. "I don't know how prosecutors are going to want to handle this. Obviously, he is at the end of his life. I doubt this ever sees the inside of a courtroom. But we need to get everything buttoned up so at least the families of the victims can have some closure."

"What should *I* do?" Fitz asked.

"What should you do?" Claire asked. "Just stand there looking smug. It's what you do best."

The mood in the room was starting to grow more light-hearted. Whatever tension there was between Kiko and Violet had smoothed over, and Claire knew it could be dealt with. Things weren't perfect, but they had just caught the Interstate Reaper, and it was starting to strike Claire how big a deal this would be when it came out in the press.

The intercom phone in the center of the table buzzed. Kathy.

Her voice was urgent. "Can you pull up Channel 4 in Portland? Or really any network. ABC, NBC, CBS. It hasn't hit the cable channels yet, but it will."

"What is it?" Claire asked.

"It's... Just turn it on," Kathy said. "You'll want to see it."

Claire's ears seemed to have stopped working because her eyes were stuck on the screen. Violet had pulled up the local news station livestream up on her computer and was casting it to the large screen on the wall.

The news scroll on the bottom of the page made Claire's chest tighten.

59-year-old sex worker Barbara Stanwich strangled and left near Sturgeon Lake outside of Portland

The footage on the screen showed a tranquil lake surrounded by trees. She tuned back in to listen to the news anchor's words.

"A grizzly scene this morning at Sturgeon Lake as police recovered the body of Portland resident Barbara Stanwich from a patch of brambles about ten yards from the water. Indications are that the murder may connect to a long-dormant serial killer dubbed The Interstate Reaper. On your screen you'll see a note left at the scene, acquired by this network from an anonymous law enforcement source."

A single piece of yellow notebook paper appeared on screen. On it were scrawled two short sentences.

I've been gone for too long, and I'm back. She was a nuisance, and now she will stare at the water forever.

CHAPTER TWENTY-FIVE

THE DAY MAMA died was hot, and I'd woken to the sound of swamp cranes fishing for frogs. They usually came at the end of the summer when the frogs were at their fattest.

I remember looking out my window from my second-story bedroom that morning and seeing them hunting. Stalking the edge of the water before thrusting their long beaks down into the murky brown. Most of the time they missed. But occasionally they came up with a fat frog between their beaks.

I often wished I was the crane and my mama was the frog. I fantasized about it many times.

When I woke up that day, I didn't know another crane was on his way to our little house.

Before he arrived, the day went like any other.

I was sixteen now, and doing all of the cooking. Mama had made me get a job at the little cafe in town and at first I only worked weekends. And then on weekdays too after she took me out of school to "homeschool" me.

For us, homeschooling meant me doing all the chores around the house while she stayed in her room drinking gin or Bayou Moonshine and watching TV or reading the Bible. The same one she had beaten me with many times. I don't know what made her turn from beating me with sticks to beating me with the Bible, but I was sixteen now and I was getting ready to leave.

She didn't know it, but I wasn't going to stay. Turned out, by the end of that day I *had* to leave.

I had done my chores around the house, cooked her breakfast, and prepared her lunch, and I was getting ready to go do a four-hour shift of washing dishes at the cafe when I heard a car kicking up gravel as it came down our driveway.

My cousin hadn't been to the house in months, or maybe it had been a year by now. I don't know, but I always loved the sound of that gravel. I ran out to the porch to meet him, but by the time I got there, mama was already there, sitting in a rocking chair and scowling.

And I knew why. He'd gotten a new red truck, a 1968 Ford F-100 half-ton.

I swear it was the most beautiful thing that had ever been on my mama's property. And I knew how much she hated it, hated him for owning it. For having the money to own it.

I ran down the steps and greeted the car as it parked. He got out and gave me a hug.

That was when mama first spoke. "You rotten little bastards. I always knew you were rotten. Like the old oak tree behind the swamp. Rotten to the core. And I don't want to be standing near you when your rotten trunk buckles and you crush everything beneath you as you fall."

We didn't mind being called rotten little bastards. We were used to it; we'd been called that and worse. As I pulled away from the hug, though, mama was standing, and I'd never seen this particular look on her face.

She took two steps down and kicked some gravel toward us. "You're a big city guy now, huh? Too big for us littleuns? Too rich, huh?" She knelt down and picked up a small stone, then walked slowly to the side of the truck without taking her eyes off him.

He tried to stand tall, but he stepped out of her way as she pressed the stone into the side of the truck and scraped it as she moved towards him. It made a screeching sound, ripping off a line of paint in its wake. I saw my cousin swallow hard, and I wished I was the crane again.

I wished *he* was the crane. Mama was older now, and fatter, too, like those frogs at the end of summer.

She had her eyes on both of us and stepped slowly backward as she scraped the rock along the truck again and again.

The sound was excruciating, but what came out of her mouth next was, somehow, even worse. "I've always known about you two. Sick and twisted and disgusting. Against God. Against everything. Conspiring against me. Fornicating. You two sick, twisted evil spirits."

She threw the rock on the ground, then picked up another one—a larger one—and smashed it against a rear taillight.

My cousin flinched and squeezed my hand tight. I squeezed back.

Mama smashed the other taillight. "For the sins you two have committed, I will not be judged. It is you two, you two sick, twisted, evil spirits." She threw the rock on the ground. "And I smite thee for I will not be judged."

I looked up at my cousin and saw something I'd never seen before in him. I'd always known him to be weak, timid. Not the crane. But that day I watched him become the crane.

Without a word, he let go of my hand and took off his belt. With four long strides he reached the back of the truck and kicked mama in the back of her leg. She fell forward, her head striking the bumper hard. It was streaked with blood.

By the time I got around to the back of the truck, my cousin already had the belt around her neck.

He was tightening it, tightening it more.

"What are you doing?" I asked.

He didn't speak. Just tightened the belt, sweating and grimacing as he held her down and pulled harder and harder.

Not a sound came out of mama's mouth as she died.

An hour later I stood under the rotten old oak tree, next to mama, whom my cousin had positioned to look out at the little pond. He told me a story then, about how when he was six he'd left the toilet seat up and she'd made him sit out there all night for the first time, using the light of the moon to count how many bugs were in the pond.

She'd told him she'd drown him if he miscounted or fell asleep.

Ever after, he'd been terrified.

But not anymore. "I wish I could leave her sitting here forever," he said. "Just staring at the water like she made me do. Just staring forever."

His voice was far away, and I knew something in him was gone, but something new had taken its place. "You are wrong," he said to her. "You *will* be judged." And then he rolled her body down into the water.

I was in shock, I know that now. But I was also hopeful that over the coming weeks the cranes would pick at her corpse and I wouldn't have to see her body if I went to the edge of the pond.

But it turned out I left that day and never came back to the house.

And it also turned out that cranes prefer to catch their prey and eat them alive.

CHAPTER TWENTY-SIX

CLAIRE FELT herself moving toward the screen, reading the note and re-reading it, eyes widening in horror. Her mouth was dry; she couldn't speak.

Fitz never seemed to run into that problem. "It's a copycat," he said definitively.

"Has to be a copycat," Kiko agreed.

"It doesn't *have* to be," Jack said.

"Everybody quiet," Claire said. "Let me think."

A thousand scenarios were racing through her mind. Of course, it *could* be a copycat, but what if they had been on the wrong track the entire time? No, that wasn't possible. They had Cunningham dead to rights—using the *little nuisance* phrase, threatening residents, not to mention he had photos of all five known victims and his bio matched the killings perfectly.

There *were* other possible explanations, like...

She didn't have time to complete the thought because she heard a commotion in the hallway. Hurrying to the door, she opened it, only to see Rivera rushing down the hall with three women as Hightower trailed behind him, making a rare appearance on their floor.

"That's her," Jonathan said, pointing at Claire.

A young woman, no older than thirty, had tears running down her cheeks. "You did this. You brought this to light." Her voice growled its way through her crying.

"Hold on," Hightower said, catching up to Rivera and the three women.

"What's going on?" Claire asked. The others joined her in the hallway, careful to stand a good couple feet behind her.

"These are the children and grandchildren of Caroline Smith," Rivera said, his tone haughty. "The fourth victim of The Interstate Reaper. They've been traumatized by the coverage of the Interstate Reaper that your team has brought back into the news. They called to complain and were routed to me. I was *happy* to bring them in to let them speak their mind. We've also had calls from relatives of Susan Swanson. Your work on this case is not only useless, it's retraumatizing the victims. These families do not deserve to be subjected to your very public and extremely futile excavation. And now it's led to a copycat! *Her* blood is on *your* hands, Agent Anderson."

"Jonathan!" Hightower's voice bellowed across the hallway and offered no room for interruption. Everyone went quiet, looking in his direction.

"Agent Greene," Hightower continued, a little more quietly, "please show these women out of the facility as gently as possible."

As Kiko led the women down the hall, one of them looked back briefly at Claire and let out a pitiful moan, but she continued her exit.

Hightower turned back to Jonathan, "I need *you* to leave this facility immediately. Didn't anyone ever teach you that people in glass houses shouldn't throw stones. Stay home, I will speak with you tomorrow over the phone."

Jonathan turned on his heels and walked away.

"Claire," Hightower continued, "get back in your office and take a beat. In ten minutes, both of you..." He waved a hand in the direction of the team standing behind her. "*All* of you... and Kiko, when she returns, meet me upstairs."

CHAPTER TWENTY-SEVEN

TWO HOURS LATER, a cold wind whipped Claire's hair across her face, a sensation she hated, but somehow felt she deserved.

She sat on the top deck of the ferry, which would take her from Edmonds, just a little north of Seattle, back to Kingston where she lived. Most days she chose to sit in her car to get some work done, but now she watched the seagulls land on the railings of the moving ferry, then take off again into the sky.

Despite the choppy internet service on the ferry, she'd spent the last ten minutes distracting herself with online shopping. Using various apps, she'd purchased a new espresso maker and a few bottles of wine on her phone. It hadn't helped her mood.

She knew that some people drank to get away from their problems, like Fitz. Some took pills or other drugs, like Fitz had once upon a time. Some became ultra-aggressive or worked out to the extreme. Claire figured Jack was probably like this. Others liked to zone out in front of Netflix when they were stressed. She pegged Violet as this type. Still others lost themselves in other people—social situations, boyfriends or girlfriends, or, at the extreme, they even became sex addicts. She hoped Kiko was the more modest of this sort.

Everyone had their coping mechanisms, and Claire had long known that the occasional distraction by way of retail therapy was hers.

But she never allowed it to go on long.

The meeting with Hightower and her team hadn't been any fun, but it had been a picnic compared to the guilt that had hit her when the children and grandchildren of Caroline Smith had appeared in the hall. She'd been oblivious to all the online coverage their investigation would stir up, but she should have known. One post from Lydia Ramirez had set off a firestorm of speculation and, within twenty-four hours, journalists were writing about the case again.

She tried not to take it personally, but there was no doubt that her actions had led directly to those women's tears. And that was the least of it. There were no clear answers, but it appeared likely that the media coverage of the Interstate Reaper had led to a copycat emerging.

There had always been a lot of online interest in the case, and many of the details were widely known. So it wasn't a stretch to imagine that the recent spate of coverage had led to a renewed interest.

Violet could verify this; the number of mentions of the Interstate Reaper case had gone up by a thousand percent over the last few days. And it was easy to imagine someone who had the capability of killing seeing the coverage and being 'inspired' to show up in Portland and commit the heinous crime.

Local police had locked down the scene, and two FBI agents whom Jack was familiar with had headed out to begin the investigation. The S.W.O.R.D. team would join them tomorrow. But for now, Claire needed to just feel miserable for a moment.

The crowd was fairly light on the top deck of the ferry. Claire stood in surprise when she saw an orange and white corgi emerge from around the corner. The little dog was racing from person to person to sniff them and allow them to pet her briefly.

She thought of Thomas Austin, a well known detective turned private investigator turned detective, who lived only twenty minutes from her. He had a loveable little corgi, but the person who emerged around the corner trailing after the dog, with its slipped collar and leash in her hand, was not Austin. It was a young woman, maybe in her early to mid twenties and, upon closer inspection, it wasn't Run, Austin's corgi. But this little one would make for a top-ranking Run doppelganger.

As she watched, the dog moved towards her. A young couple laughed loudly when it jumped deftly backwards out of arm's reach when they bent down to try to give her a hug.

Claire waited for her turn and the little dog came up, sniffed at her shoe, and jumped back just as Claire's scratch behind the ear might transition into a scruff nabbing. Claire watched as the dog disappeared around another corner, wondering how Austin would handle a situation like hers, a case like this.

Austin was one of the people who had convinced her not to retire, to stay on the job. She couldn't resent him for it. If staying had been a mistake, it wasn't *his* fault. The truth was, she wished she could get his advice. She needed a neutral third party. But she was never one to ask for help. Instead, she just walked to the front of the ferry and stood there, letting the wind batter her face.

As the ferry slowed, Kingston came into view. She could even make out her house, which was less than a mile from the ferry dock as the crow flies, right on the water. She knew Benny was there, and that being with him would lighten her mood.

One way or another, she had to get her head back in the game.

Tomorrow morning she would be in Portland, and she had no idea where this investigation would take Task Force S.W.O.R.D. next.

CHAPTER TWENTY-EIGHT

"OKAY BROS, today I've got to tell you about a new game that isn't even on the market yet. But I got early access, and I'm here to tell you, it is *utterly* lit."

Claire listened through the door as Benny recorded a video for his YouTube channel. She wasn't eavesdropping; she was being cautious. She had once knocked loudly while he was three-quarters of the way through what he called *my most baller video ever*, and she'd ruined it. He had to start over from the beginning. So now she made sure to listen for the enthusiastic and somewhat performative tone he used in his videos, and she only knocked when he seemed to have finished.

"So, guys, this game, *Memory Mind*, it's like nothing you've seen before! Imagine mixing a super cool memory training app with the adventure vibes of an RPG like *Zelda*. So, you start off in this mystical world, right? And each quest you complete, you gotta solve puzzles and remember patterns to level up. It's not just about battling monsters; it's about training your brain!" Claire heard the canned sound effect of an explosion and, in her mind's eye, she could see the animated expression Benny's face would be making at the camera to convey that his brain was exploding. "Bros, each level gets trickier. And the bosses? They challenge your memory in crazy ways. You literally can't defeat them unless you've sharpened your skills." The canned sound effect of a pencil in an electric sharpener played. "It's epic, totally immersive, and it seriously tests your brain power. Here, lemme show you..."

He paused for a long time, and Claire knew that meant it was safe to knock. He recorded his videos in small segments, and the break meant that he was going to splice in scenes from the video game, over which he would narrate the action.

Benny opened the door a moment later, greeting her with a big hug.

A good portion of her stress melted away. She'd read a few books about not sweating the small stuff and not taking work too seriously, but she found it easy to forget the strategies they taught when faced with the sorts of mental, emotional, and sometimes physical stresses she dealt with on a daily basis.

"Hey Bean-Bean," she said, "I love that pencil sharpener sound effect, *bro*."

"Ewe, mom. Don't say bro. But, thanks, bro."

"Your video clips are sounding more professional every day. It seems like you're working hard to level up *Down To Game*. Please excuse the pun."

"I can't say it yet on the video because it's not official, but they want to pay me to promote their games."

Claire frowned. "Is that honest work? Won't your viewers resent that?"

"No, it's just part of the YouTube thing, mom. As long as my reviews are honest, it's okay. They won't pay me much but—pro tip—always ask about compensation."

Claire wasn't so sure about this, but she wasn't going to object. She trusted her son, but she was also too tired to think.

"Want to play some *Fish Wars II?*" Benny asked.

"Yes." Fortunately, playing *Fish Wars II* required zero mental effort.

"I think after multiple weeks of playing, you might actually be able to hit a motionless target. After you master that, the NPC fish had better watch their gills." He laughed loudly, which made Claire laugh, too.

They headed downstairs. Benny sat in front of the television on the floor and got the controllers ready and Claire made a bowl of popcorn to share before sitting beside him to play.

Ten minutes into gaming, Benny flipped his controller onto the floor playfully. "ARGH, Mom, you are the single worst video game player on this planet and quite possibly others that have not yet been discovered."

"Are you saying I'm an embarrassment to Earth?"

"That would be too generous."

They played for half an hour more. Claire didn't hit any intended targets, but she managed to drop an extra reel for Benny to pick up when he broke his due to overfishing. Never mind that their characters nearly starved to death as she scrambled with the controller to figure out how to access her inventory.

While playing, Claire ignored three more texts from Chris Thacker. A quick scan revealed they had nothing to do with the case. Instead, they were increasingly odd, inappropriate, even desperate dinner invitations.

And by the time they were done, Claire was deeply regretting her brief flirtation with the man.

~

Later, after tucking Benny into bed, Claire sat alone in her office, staring at the unusual map of Washington State marked with a shiny red star on the town of Moses Lake. It was where she had been born, and where her parents had died along with dozens of other members of a cult in a mass suicide.

She'd been the only survivor.

Her uncle had given her the map the day he told her about her parent's death. It was an encaustic collage. The geographical features were a mishmash of raw materials— string, different types of paper, some areas painted or colored in as though the artist had used a crayon. All of the labels for places, symbols, and icons were in different fonts and sizes, having been torn from varied text sources. Her uncle had told her that every element of the map was unique and beautiful, just like her. He gifted her the piece and told her—*If only one tree survives a forest fire, all it needs to do is stand there and keep growing.*

Maybe it was because the relatives of the victims had been so distraught at having their past traumas resurfaced, but Claire's thoughts of her own history were niggling at her mind.

She'd done a little research in the past, but hadn't gotten far. The line of inquiry was emotionally exhausting and somewhere between growing up, getting married, having children, and all the trappings of being an adult, she'd never found the time to dive into that quagmire. Tonight, she felt she wouldn't be able to stand in her life and keep growing until she got some answers. What did that cult mean to her parents? And what did the cult mean to its leader? Why had they all taken their own lives? Why had she survived? *How* had she survived?

Claire's phone began vibrating on the desk, and she was

surprised to see Simone Aoki's name pop up on the caller ID.

She'd met Sy briefly during a recent case where she'd worked alongside the Kitsap Sheriff's Department. Sy was an NCIS agent on the east coast, but hadn't even been involved in the case. Claire had heard she was still dating Thomas Austin even though she'd returned home.

She took a small sip of her wine before answering. "Hello?"

"Claire," Sy said, "I hope it's not too late."

Claire glanced at the clock on her desk. It was only 9:45, but that meant it was nearly 1:00 AM in Sy's timezone.

"Not at all," Claire said, "Are you still running on West Coast time?"

"Nah," Sy said. "I've just been up too late, ruminating, I guess."

"Well..." Claire stammered. She wasn't used to receiving calls out of the blue and was still a bit disoriented. "How are things?"

"Well, you know that Austin and I have been dating," Sy said. "I spent a few weeks out there and we've gotten pretty close now. Anyway, I'm hoping to get your advice."

Claire laughed. "If you're looking for dating advice, you've called the wrong woman. I'm recently divorced, not really dating, and yet somehow I seem to have attracted a man who is either just awkward or will turn out to be my stalker."

"Oh no!"

Claire laughed again. "Maybe he's just a bad texter. I heard about this mother-daughter relationship experiment where some mothers texted and others spoke over the phone with their daughters. The daughters who heard their mother's voices had significantly higher oxytocin and much lower cortisol levels than those that interacted via text."

"That tracks," Sy said. "Communicating via text, it's like you can forget there's a person at the other end. I'm lucky, Austin isn't much of a technophile."

"No, he isn't," Claire said, swirling her cabernet in the glass. "My guy is a handsome nurse practitioner. Seemed perfectly normal. And yet, he sent me a few over-the-top texts after meeting me for a few minutes." Claire sighed. "Is that weird?"

"Indeed it is. Trust your gut, and be careful with yourself."

"Wait. How did this conversation go from you calling me for dating advice to me telling you about *my* amorous knots."

"Don't worry, Claire, I wasn't really calling for dating advice."

"Wise."

"I'm thinking about moving to Washington. But I don't have any female friends out there. Austin is great, but he hasn't lived in Washington for long and besides, I can't just move there for him. Women need other women in their lives. I know you grew up in Washington, so I thought I'd bend your ear if you're up for it."

Claire sipped her wine. "Absolutely. Consider us officially girlfriends."

"Thanks. Anyway, there are a few reasons I might be coming west, it's not only to be near Austin. How is it living out there?"

"Well," Claire said, "here on the Western side, the summers are more beautiful than anywhere I've ever been, the springs and falls are brief, and the winters are extremely gray. It's almost like there are only two seasons—Summer and Gray Drizzle. If you're looking at moving to Western Washington, I guess you just have to ask yourself how you feel about being wet a good chunk of the time and how much gray your psyche can handle."

"Might be worth it for the summers. Is that what you're telling me?" Sy asked.

"Right."

"Well, I don't love gray weather, but I don't like the months of snow we get here much either."

"When are you looking to make a move?"

"I have three more months to go before I can retire. Pension won't be as good as if I stayed working until I'm sixty-two, but I'm ready to move on now."

"Cheers to your pension and congratulations on your possible retirement, Sy." Claire took a sip of her cabernet, which was delightful. The wine glass bumped against Claire's cell phone and made a ting.

"Wait a second, are you drinking a glass of wine?"

"Why yes," Claire said. "I'm imbibing my evening constitutional."

"I thought I heard the tinkling of crystal," Sy said. "You know, I'm thinking about working at a winery. I'm talking to a place in central Washington called Green Ridge Vineyards, out by Crab Creek. They make a lovely Cab for under thirty bucks a bottle."

Claire felt her chest tighten, then set down her wine.

"What did I say?" Sy asked.

Claire realized she'd gasped audibly.

"No, nothing, it's just that... I know Crab Creek. It's not far from Moses Lake. Where I... where they... where they found me." She cleared her throat. "I'm sorry. You don't even know what I'm talking about, do you?"

"Actually, I think I do," Sy said. "Austin told me about your miraculous survival. I'm so sorry you lost your parents. I didn't realize the winery was so close to your history there."

"Thank you... it was all... well, it was a long time ago, right?" Claire said.

"I really am sorry."

"Please," Claire said, "it's nothing." As she said it, she knew it wasn't true, and the silence on the line told her that Sy wasn't buying it either. "Yeah, it's *not* nothing, and I really don't want to go down this rabbit hole, I mean I *can't*. Not tonight. But sometimes I feel overwhelmed by the inexplicable horror of it all. What makes people follow a charismatic leader to a little commune in central Washington, then take their own lives and..." She felt the tears welling in her eyes. "The lives of their children? You know, there were other children there. So why did *I* make it out alive?"

"I'm sorry," Sy said. "I wish I had answers."

Claire gathered herself. Just saying it out loud had made her feel a little better, and she had the ability to set emotions aside when she wanted to. She took another sip of wine and forced herself into the present. "Anyway... I want to hear more about your plans. So, wine and wineries, huh? *This* makes your wanting to move out here make a lot more sense. Washington has some amazing wineries."

"That's what I hear," Sy said. "I've had a few very good bottles and I'm desperate to learn more."

"Oooh! I see a wine tasting tour in our future." Claire took another sip.

"I'm in," Sy said. "What's it like on the Eastern side of the state?"

"Well, I don't mean to scare you off but once you're on the other side of the mountains it's basically an inferno in the summer and a frozen tundra in the winter."

"That cold, really?"

"Well, I could be exaggerating," Claire admitted. "I don't think it's quite as cold as the East Coast." Claire felt their conversation coming to an end but wanted some feedback on another issue. Most of the women in Claire's life were either subordinates or couldn't understand the burden of her work. "Can I ask you something a bit work related?"

"Sure."

"I'm grappling with one of my investigations hurting the victims and possibly other innocent people as well. That ever happen to you?"

"That's tough. But Claire, the investigation isn't what causes pain. None of the pain is your fault. It's not up to you if what you have to do to catch the bad guy triggers grief. You have an important job to do and we all need you to do it, especially the victims past, present, and potential future."

"Thank you for that," Claire said. She'd taken in Sy's words and they'd helped. "Look at the time, Sy. You need to get some sleep."

"Thanks for taking my call tonight. Maybe if I end up out there we can start a wine club or something. Let's see, we'll call ourselves... the... uuuuh... Female Officers Cabernet Club United or something."

"The F.O.C.C.U.?" Claire felt her laugh pierce her fatigue. Spending time with Sy was going to be a blast.

"Not bad for one in the morning, right?"

"It's perfect," Claire said, "and honestly, I'm really glad you called. Reach out again when your plans for migration solidify."

CHAPTER TWENTY-NINE

"I CAN'T BELIEVE that bastard Jonathan wouldn't let us take the chopper." Jack pulsed his grip on the steering wheel, emphasizing his frustration. His knuckles popped.

That was okay with Claire. She liked Jack to be a little bit on edge. That was when he was at his best. Leaning over from the front passenger seat, she inspected the speedometer. Jack was doing ninety in a seventy-mile-per-hour zone. "At this rate, you might get us there faster than the helicopter would have."

They were halfway to Portland, normally a three-hour drive, but somewhat less at this speed.

Jack veered onto the shoulder to pass a beer truck that was only doing seventy-five.

"I just hope we don't have to pitstop in heaven first," Kiko called from the back seat of the SUV.

Although her voice sounded jovial, a glance at the rearview mirror told Claire that Kiko may have been crying recently. Claire didn't want to ask and didn't want to know, but she suspected the tears had something to do with what was going on between Kiko and Jack, and possibly Violet.

"The files arrived," Kiko said. "Plug in this aux cable." She passed forward a thin black wire, which Claire plugged into the outlet under the stereo.

Kiko continued, "The email from Violet says that this is a compilation of highlights from witness interviews that were taken throughout the investigation. She had them all digitized and sent me an MP3."

"Please tell her good work," Claire said.

Claire turned up the radio and a faint hissing sound filled the car.

"This first one is an interview conducted by Agent Stacy Wegman, the one Jack and I met with. The interviewee is Bill McKenzie, who was jogging in Bellingham at the time of the first murder. He saw a vehicle with no license plates a block or two from the scene, within an hour of the estimated time of death."

A man's voice filled the car, and it was fairly clear despite being on a recording over forty years old. "It was a tan Ford Sedan."

The interviewer, Agent Wegman, asked, "And did you get a look at the driver?"

"Long blonde hair," the witness said, "Caucasian. And fairly young."

"And which street did it turn down?"

"I was on... ummm... Eldridge Ave. Then I turned left on Nequalicum. I live on West Illinois, so I wasn't far from home."

Agent Wegman asked a series of questions about the witness's background, as though tying up loose ends.

"Pause it," Claire said to Kiko.

She did.

"I have a question for both of you," Claire continued, "what did Agent Wegman do wrong?"

Jack switched lanes to veer around a semi-truck. "She didn't follow up on the description of the witness," he said.

"And why do you think she didn't?" Claire asked.

"Sexism," Kiko said. "She assumed the killer was a man and therefore that part of this witness's testimony was not relevant."

"Exactly," Claire said. "And of course, the vast majority of serial killers *are* men, so it wasn't a ridiculous move, but still. Play the next interview."

Kiko began the recording again and skipped forward. "According to Violet, this is an interview from a local police officer in Portland. Agent Wegman was going over the evidence he had found at the scene."

"Six witnesses all saw the same car. Brown station wagon." A man's voice crackled into the soundscape. "We've got it narrowed down to just a couple models."

"Driver?" Agent Wegman asked.

"That's the update," the officer replied. "Half of them say it was a woman in her late twenties or thirties with short brown hair. Half of them say a man, possibly in his late forties, also with brown hair."

"And the witnesses saw this vehicle over what period?"

"From an hour before the murder to an hour after."

Agent Wegman sighed heavily. "That ain't much to go on, is it?"

When the officer didn't reply, Claire figured he'd shaken his head.

"Which half do you believe?" Agent Wegman asked.

"We both know witnesses are wrong most of the time. They don't know *what* the hell they saw."

Stacy chuckled. "You got that right. Could also have been two different vehicles, of course."

"I don't think so," he said. "Four of the six reported that the radio was blasting *Sweet Dreams* by the Eurythmics. The other two reported hearing some electronic or modern pop music, so we assume they heard the same song but just didn't know the artist."

"That's odd," Stacy said, "the same song for such a long period of time?"

"Right. I chalked it up to a couple just cruising and listening to their favorite cassette over and over."

"Could be," Agent Wegman said, but her next few questions didn't pursue the discrepancy any further.

Claire said, "Pause it."

Kiko paused the recording and the car went quiet.

"What did you two hear?" Claire asked.

"A man in his late forties at the time would track well with Augustus's current age," Jack said.

"What about the music?" Kiko asked. "What would your average mid-forties guy have been listening to in the spring of 1983?"

"Depends what kind of guy he is," Jack said. "If he was the kind of guy who stayed on top of pop music, probably Michael Jackson, or Prince, or Whitney Houston. Or, yeah, the Eurythmics."

"How many guys in their mid forties do you think stay on top of pop music?" Claire asked.

Jack shrugged. "Don't know many guys in their forties."

Claire knew a fair amount of men in their forties and doubted many of them listened to whatever the kids were listening to. Then again, most of them worked in the FBI, so perhaps they weren't a representative sample. "Makes me think someone younger was driving that car, I mean, when mixed with the witnesses who said as much."

"That's quite a leap," Jack said.

"I didn't say she was the *only* one driving the car." Claire paused to see if they would fill in the gaps.

Jack and Kiko were silent for a long time.

"Jack," Kiko finally said, breaking the silence. "I think we need to tell Claire."

"Let's just focus on the case," Claire said. "It's been pretty obvious that you two are dating and have total disregard for the FBI's fraternization policies. We will get into it, but not now."

"That's not what I meant," Kiko said. "It's something else. Come on Jack, we have to tell her about the lipstick."

"Okay..." Claire said, confused. "What lipstick?"

"Sanchez knew the color of lipstick," Kiko blurted. "One of the victims had used it and it was found later. He knew the color *by name* and said he got the info from Jake Whitehall. But that information had never made it out." Her voice jumped a half step and she spoke more rapidly. "He *also* knew about the positioning of the bodies, but that we might be able to chalk up to info he says he got from Whitehall, who got it from reporters who never printed it."

"If he ever even *spoke* with Whitehall," Jack said, "which I'm still not sure about."

Claire's mind raced. "You *both* kept this from the team... Why? Just... Why?"

"Fitz was—" Jack started.

"Was what? Oh, was Fitz being Fitz again?" Blood rushed to Claire's face like a hot flash. She was livid. "Your fragile ego couldn't stand to be threatened in front of your new departmental girlfriend? I—" She cut herself off. "Never mind. It's my fault. I thought there might be bumps in the road if you two were dating, but keeping crucial information from the team? Jack, pull over."

"But we need to—"

Jack couldn't finish his sentence before Claire repeated her demand.

"Pull over. Now. I need to think."

Jack pulled onto the shoulder and stopped.

Claire opened the window and let the wind hit her face. She hadn't smoked since a brief stint after college, but she wished she had a cigarette. "I've been wondering whether Augustus Cunningham had an accomplice. Maybe the two of you have already met him."

"The witnesses saw both a man and a woman driving the car," Kiko said. "If Sanchez was Cunningham's accomplice, that doesn't track at all."

"He did have a ponytail back then, and he has a slight build," Jack offered. "Maybe..."

Claire pulled out her phone and tapped out a text to Violet, whom she knew was in communication with Fitz.

In Portland soon, but tell Fitz to angle his questions in the direction of an accomplice. And Sanchez. Find out if they knew each other. And I want to know if there are any mentions of lipstick shades in any of the articles connected to the case, focus in on the shade...

"What was it called?" Claire demanded. "The lipstick shade. What was it called?"

"Garnet Devotion," Jack said.

Claire finished her text and pressed send.

"You really don't need to be here," Fitz said, and it came out even more contemptuously than he'd intended.

Chris Thacker, the ridiculously handsome nurse practitioner and director of the facility, stood in the doorway. "After what happened last time? I think I do. I'm not giving you the chance to bite him back."

Fitz liked to believe that he was comfortable in his own skin, but being around a man roughly his own age—a man who held a respectable position, whose clothes were clean and crisp, and whose physique was like something off the cover of *Handsome Healthcare Workers Monthly*—made the occasional shame he felt about his personal appearance hit him like a wave.

But he wouldn't allow himself to collapse. He'd fight back. "Fine," he said, turning his attention back to Gus. "Augustus Cunningham, do you understand and consent to the fact that I am recording this conversation and streaming it to my colleague, Special Agent Violet Wei, who is in our Seattle office?"

Cunningham turned, opened his mouth to speak, then nodded slowly, saying nothing.

"Let the record reflect that the patient, Mr. Cunningham, has nodded," Fitz said. "Doc, do you agree?"

Thacker said loudly, "I do. He has nodded consent."

Fitz generally didn't like to record things, partially because it made people self-conscious and partially because he was worried that he'd do something he didn't want on the record. But Violet had convinced him to stream the conversation from his cell phone, which had an amplifying microphone attached to it. That way, she could run the conversation through various voice analyzers to figure out whether there was anything to be learned from Cunningham's inflections. She had described it as "like a lie detector test that actually works, on steroids." She could also compare the recording to the audio clip from the Yreka crime scene, but that was just a formality. Fitz had no doubt it was Cunningham.

"Are you aware, Mr. Cunningham," Fitz began, "that a woman was murdered yesterday, and that the killer claims to be the Interstate Reaper, claims to be responsible for the murders you have all but admitted to."

Fitz felt Dr. Thacker's eyes on him, but tried to block the Adonis out. He was finding it difficult.

Although most of his mind was focused on the task at

hand, something had been eating away at Fitz like an invisible mite gnawing his flesh.

Why had he become so aggressive about this man's texts to Claire? Sure, he respected Claire, and of course, she was attractive. When Kiko had asked him during their first case whether there had ever been anything between them, he had answered honestly. No, there hadn't been. Until very recently, Claire was a married woman and, even though he saw himself as an amoral person, he did respect marriage—for whatever reason.

He never even tried pursuing her. But he knew himself well enough to notice that, during that conversation with Kiko, he hadn't been fully honest. And that Kiko hadn't asked the right question. No, there *hadn't* been anything between them, but Fitz was starting to realize that some piece of him had often wished there could be.

Fitz heard Violet's voice in his ear. "Is Cunningham responding? If so, I can't hear him."

"No," Fitz said. "He's not responding yet."

"Claire texted me, something about lipstick, and how she thinks there may have been an accomplice all along."

"Crikey," Fitz whispered sarcastically. "Why didn't *I* think of that?" An accomplice was one of a dozen possibilities that had occurred to Fitz. He assumed Jack had gotten in Claire's ear and tried to convince her that Sanchez was indeed involved. Fitz wasn't buying it. No way the man before him had a male accomplice roughly twenty-five years his junior. "And Violet, please stay out of my ear if you can. I need to lock in here." He turned back to Cunningham. "Gus, how does it make you feel that there is a copycat out there?"

Cunningham didn't respond.

"I am wondering," Fitz continued, standing up and looking out the window, "about the water. This new victim was also found on the water. I wonder what it signifies? What does it mean?"

Fitz glanced down. Cunningham hadn't moved from his chair. It wasn't that he had gone comatose or fallen asleep. His eyes were darting around, and Fitz knew that he'd heard and, despite his dementia, even understood him.

"Taylor," Fitz said, "I'm wondering about Taylor as well."

"Keep that name out of your filthy mouth!" The words came as a hiss from Cunningham's barely open lips.

Fitz sat and met his eyes. "Taylor," he said again, "it *is* Taylor, right? Not Sailor?"

Cunningham said nothing, but Fitz saw the recognition in his eyes. Even though his mind was only partially there, something in his eyes felt alive and dangerous.

And it was exactly where Fitz wanted him to be.

CHAPTER THIRTY

"I WONDER," Fitz said, "why would saying a single word—Taylor—make you so angry? What single word could someone say that would make *my* eyes burn like that? All I can think about is that it must be something about a woman." Fitz shook his head. "I guess *Taylor* could be a woman's name *or* a man's name. I am assuming you are heterosexual, is that correct?"

Cunningham didn't answer.

"Well, regardless," Fitz continued, "let's say Taylor *is* a woman. You are around the right age that maybe you fell in love with Elizabeth Taylor, as did many who came of age around your time."

His eyes had gone vacant again, but now he was blinking rapidly.

Fitz was about to launch into another tirade when Thacker interrupted him. "Mr. Pembroke, please lean away from Mr. Cunningham. You're being too aggressive. Despite what he may have done, he is still a patient in our facility. And this is a place of healing."

Fitz shot him a dismissive look, but leaned back as

directed. "Yes," he continued, "it must be a woman's name. But in all the files, we found nothing about a Taylor. We saw nothing about marriages or children, we found no love interests. Our agents did a pretty good job back in the eighties, and yet not a single mention of a Taylor, man *or* woman."

Fitz noticed Cunningham's hands, which were on the armrests on either side of his wheelchair. They were shaking.

"Do you have any kids?" he asked.

Cunningham shook his head. "No."

"He speaks at last! And you were attracted to women?"

"I'm not queer," Cunningham spat, "never was."

"Okay, well we don't exactly use that term anymore," Fitz said, "but okay."

Cunningham looked out the window. "There was someone."

"Taylor?" Fitz asked.

"I saved her." Cunningham began to hum a tune Fitz almost recognized and then, oddly, began to sing. "*I'm not going to miss you...*"

"Who?" Fitz asked. "Who do you not miss? Was it Taylor? Your mother, another woman?"

"I saved her. I saved her."

There was a long pause, and Violet filled it with words in Fitz's earpiece. "Based on the vocal analysis so far, the fluctuations in Cunningham's tone and pitch, particularly when he said 'I saved her,' align closely with patterns we've observed in truthful recollections. The AI is cross-referencing these vocal characteristics against millions of hours of recorded interrogations and personal narratives. It can discern stress levels, which are currently high, possible deception, which is low, and emotional connection to certain subjects. What's interesting here is the emotional intensity—it spikes in a way that's consistent with genuine, emotionally charged memories. This suggests that whatever he's saying about this 'her' who he saved genuinely connects those memories with significant emotional truth. And the song he's singing is a Glen Campbell tune which, interestingly, Glen Cambell wrote for his family when he learned he had dementia."

"Is Taylor the one you saved?" Fitz asked.

"I don't know," Cunningham said.

Fitz considered this. It was the first time Cunningham had said those words. Fitz knew, of course, that there were many things Cunningham didn't know. But the fact that he admitted to not knowing meant that he knew that there *was* an accurate answer to the question.

"Tell me about when you saved this person. Tell me what you did."

Cunningham closed his eyes and began slowly shaking his head. "Crane. She said I was the crane."

Fitz heard Thacker take a step forward, but he held up a hand like a crossing guard signaling for cars to stop.

Thacker stopped.

Cunningham shook his head faster and then faster still.

"We need to stop this," Thacker said.

"*I'm not going to miss you...*" Cunningham sang.

"No," Fitz said. "Gus. Augustus Cunningham. Tell me what you did when you saved her. When you saved this girl or this woman."

"Girl," Cunningham said, "Taylor was a girl. A young woman. She said I was the crane."

Fitz heard Violet in his ears. "Again, the timbre of his voice aligns with a deep personal and truthful connection to the subject. Short version: he's telling the truth, at least as he understands it. You'd have to think that a man who puts

Glen Campbell lyrics to memory, no matter his past, would be sincere."

"Was she your little sister," Fitz asked, "or perhaps a friend?"

Head still shaking violently, Cunningham spat, "Here little cousin. Here kitty, kitty. Shhhhhh.... Shhhhhhh, not a nuisance." He brought his hands up to his chest suddenly, as though he'd been struck in the sternum.

Fitz felt it, too. A pain in his chest.

He didn't need Violet to tell him that Cunningham was emotionally connected to his subject. Fitz himself could feel it. And he could feel whatever pain Cunningham was going through, too. It was as though Fitz himself had disappeared, merged with the empty space in the room, and was now absorbing all the decades of pain that resided in Cunningham.

Fitz felt himself tearing up, as though at a movie in which the pain of love lost is perfectly transmitted through the screen. "You loved her," Fitz said, his own voice breaking.

"Enough!" Thacker said. "This is becoming dangerous. I'm ordering you to stop this interview."

Fitz ignored him.

Cunningham's head was still shaking violently, and now Fitz's own head shook, too, as though he was trying to become Cunningham, to feel every bit of him.

"If you won't stop," Thacker said. "I'm going to get security."

Fitz ignored him.

He heard Thacker hurrying away and turned back to Cunningham.

CHAPTER THIRTY-ONE

IT WAS late morning by the time they arrived in Portland, and the air was sticky and hot as Claire got out of the car. She'd arranged to meet the most promising witness in the case, a sixty-five-year-old man named America Jackson, who lived in a tent encampment just off the highway.

Kiko and Jack had both stayed fairly quiet during the drive, and Claire hadn't pressed the matter any further. Violet was looking into the lipstick angle and had double-checked that Sanchez was still stashed away safely at the SeaTac Federal Detention Center.

Claire had also made a few calls, including one to the FBI agent on the scene in Portland, who warned her that Mr. Jackson was, to say the least, an *interesting* character. The homeless man indicated that he had crucial information to share but, when brought in for an interview, had been disinclined to share it. The visit had cost the department two sandwiches and three cups of coffee. Claire hoped to have better luck on his home turf.

When she saw that turf, she told Jack and Kiko to wait

in the car, figuring that a one-on-one would be less intimidating and yield more information.

Jackson's home consisted of three tents, each ingeniously rigged from a collage of materials that might have once had other lives: a patchwork of canvas from old billboards, faded tarpaulins that flapped lightly in the breeze, even a repurposed sail either stolen or discarded from a boat.

The smallest tent was off to the left side and was surrounded by a makeshift garden of container plants—tomatoes, peppers, and even a stout lemon tree in a half-barrel. The largest tent seemed to serve as the living area, its interior visible through a makeshift door draped with a beaded curtain that clinked softly with each passing gust.

Claire found Jackson in the middle tent, a kitchen area equipped with pots and pans hanging from a metal tent frame and a small gas stove that looked like it had been salvaged from a camper van. Herbs hung drying from the frame, releasing a pungent, earthy aroma that mingled with the scent of coffee brewing on the stove.

"Mr. Jackson," Claire said, standing just outside the open flap. "Claire Anderson, FBI."

Cars whooshed by on the highway as he turned.

"Oh, okay! So you're the men in black they told me they'd be sending, huh? The suits and ties don't fool me, Mr. G-man! You're all just puppeteers in a grand cosmic farce, and I'm not falling for it, not one bit!"

Claire couldn't help but smile.

Jackson poured himself a cup of coffee and turned to face her. "Let's start with your little UFO shindig, shall we? Area 51? Maybe you've heard of it. I *knoooow* what's tucked away in those hangars, and so do you, I'm betting. Back in the Reagan years, while I was jamming to Billy Idol and Cyndi Lauper, you folks were busy hosting intergalactic tea parties. But guess what? I've got my own satellite dishes, made from good ol' readily available aluminum foil, baked and tested. I'm catching whispers from the cosmos and you're not fooling anyone!"

Jackson's complexion hinted at diverse heritage, his curly hair a blend of salt and pepper, closely cropped to his head, contrasting with his long, bushy beard, which was meticulously groomed and flecked with gray. And he was dressed surprisingly well for someone residing off the beaten path—a crisply ironed shirt under a well-worn, embroidered leather vest with stitching that looked like it had stories of its own.

"I don't know about any of that," Claire said, "but I do know that a woman was murdered and that you may have information about that. Local police said you may have seen the abduction."

"Sure I have information, but why in the name of Safria, Queen of the Cosmos would I give it to *this* government? You turn us into mindless zombies with your Wi-Fi signals and 5G frequencies. I see them, the lost souls, wandering the streets—I know a brainwash epidemic when I see one. It's not just a pandemic; the mucky-mucks want this thing to go full bore intergalactic contagion, man. So no, Mrs. FBI Agent, I *won't* spill my beans. Because you're just dying to get them planted so you can climb the bean-pole past the clouds in search of the next species to infect! You can go stuff your badges and your questions. I'm keeping my eyes wide open and my mouth shut tight! Nobody's getting a chance to plant my magic beans, nobody, nohow!"

Claire said, "That's too bad. I brought someone who can address your concerns. She's read your letters and has answers for you." She waited until he met her eyes. "Mr. Jackson, I'm here to make a deal."

He plucked a sprig of rosemary from a branch that hung off a metal tent pole. "You're lying me up."

Claire held up both hands. "Okay, fine... but, so you know, she doesn't show up for just anyone."

She turned to leave.

"Wait," Jackson said. "*Who* doesn't show up?"

Claire turned back. "Special Agent Vivian Greene of the joint FBI-NASA-CIA-Secret Service Task Force. She wants to know what you know—*how* you know what you know—and she's willing to trade classified information for it." She paused, letting her lies sink in. She wasn't the performer Kiko was, but hoped she'd sounded convincing enough. "Would you like to meet Agent Greene? Are you ready for the truth, America Jackson?"

He folded his arms. "I'll listen to what she has to say."

"I have something new." Violet was in Fitz's ear again.

"*Shhh!*" He was on a roll and couldn't stand to be interrupted.

"You loved Taylor," Fitz said to Cunningham. "And she... *she* is the reason you started killing. You saved her."

"It's something *about* Taylor," Violet insisted. Fitz ripped out the earpiece and tucked it into his breast pocket.

"She," Cunningham repeated. "She is the reason..."

The old man's head fell back and his mouth went agape, displaying rampant oral decay. The sound that came out of him next was like nothing Fitz had ever heard. A guttural scream, a cry so ancient it might have risen from the earth itself. It was as though Cunningham had gathered the pain of all the world, held it within himself for ninety years, and was just now letting it out in one breath.

Fitz felt tears rolling down his own cheeks. He slapped

himself in the face, trying to regain composure. But he couldn't. As Cunningham's scream continued, he felt the pain echoing through his entire body.

In a flash, he realized that the pain Cunningham was feeling about Taylor was the same Fitz felt about Claire. He'd been covering it up for years—with jokes, with sarcasm, with aggressive psychological analysis, with deflection, and with more than his fair share of lagers.

He'd been ignoring them, but now his feelings were here, like the chaotic winds of a sudden storm, whipping decaying leaves through a dark forest.

Fitz lost control.

All along, Claire had been *Fitz's* Beatrice. He'd been wading through hell, holding onto a hope unseen even to him. Burying his moral shortcomings beneath his greatest object of pride, his intellect, he'd been unconsciously hoping that this would be enough to win Claire's admiration at least, but ideally her affection.

Cunningham's eyes closed and his head fell forward. Fitz leaned in, thinking he'd passed out—or worse.

When Fitz felt for a pulse, Cunningham's eyes opened wide. Then Cunningham lunged forward, mouth wide.

Fitz roared in pain as the man's front teeth bit into his ear.

CHAPTER THIRTY-TWO

BACK AT THE SUV, Claire found Jack leaning on the hood and squinting down at his phone. "Any luck?" he asked without looking up.

Kiko got out and joined them.

"No luck yet," Claire said to both of them. "But Kiko, can you pretend to be a special agent from a joint CIA-FBI-NASA-Secret Service Task Force who is here to answer some questions about conspiracy theories? I guessed that he'd written letters to various agencies, and apparently I guessed right."

"Can I?" she asked. "There's nothing I'd enjoy more. Any background intel you can give me?"

"Let's see," Claire said. "He has beans. Doesn't want to spill them because humans are a vector for intergalactic brainwashing."

"Sounds accurate," Kiko said.

"And, of course, there's tinfoil."

"Right," Kiko said. "I got this."

Jack held up his phone. "Violet just wrote to us. She has something. It wasn't in any of the files, but she was doing research on Augustus Cunningham's background and found out that his high school mascot was named *Taylor the Gator*."

"Hmm," Claire said, "not a person."

It wasn't what she'd expected, and she wondered whether *Taylor* was Cunningham's *Rosebud*, the sled from Citizen Kane. Maybe he had fond high school memories of playing sports or sitting in the stands. Before everything in his life went to hell.

"She is calling the school and finding out anything else she can," Jack continued.

"Good," Claire said. "Jack, keep up with Violet's info reconnaissance, the school, the lipstick, anything new on Sanchez. Kiko, you and I are going to see if we can convince this guy we're on his side of the intergalactic information wars."

Thankfully, Kiko was already dressed for the role.

She wore a black skirt suit adorned with a silver flower pin. Her dreadlocks were tied back into a ponytail, and by the time she walked into Jackson's tent, she'd put on a pair of thick glasses, which made her look five years older, and had pinched her face in a way that made her look like she'd aged another five due to stress.

"Mr. Jackson," she began, "let me start off by saying this, we don't just go around giving out the truth to people. Not everything in your letters was correct, but enough of it was that you've been on my radar for three years. We're just here to fill in the blanks. Truth is, we need you, but what is also true is, you need us." Kiko folded her arms. "And I'm prepared to convince you of this."

Claire was impressed. She would have loved to see Kiko in an improv class.

"This is how it's going to go," Kiko continued. "You are going to give me information about what you saw the other day. For each solid fact you give me, I will let you ask one question and I will give you an honest answer. Shake on it?" She held out her hand. "If you choose not to, we are fully prepared to erase your memory of this conversation as well as many of the memories you hold dear." She paused for effect. "That's the deal, take it or leave it."

Jackson reached out a hand. "I'll take the deal," he said.

For the next twenty minutes, they went back and forth, Jackson giving details about what he'd seen the morning of the murder and Kiko, for her part, answering his questions. Of course, nearly everything she said was nonsense, but America Jackson believed every word.

Her validation skills were top tier—a slight tilt of the head, a facial expression, a knowing nod. She knew exactly when to confirm his assertions, and when to deny them to retain credibility. A man like Jackson would never believe that she would show up and admit to *all* the conspiracies. But she also knew that a mind like his wanted so badly to know the truth, that he would cling onto any scrap she provided.

But more importantly, during the interview a picture of the day of the murder became clear in Claire's head.

Jackson was well-known in the homeless community, riding an electric bicycle from encampment to encampment and from rest area to rest area. He called himself a "Minister of Truth," and would often provide water bottles and even food to other homeless people in exchange for their willingness to listen to him. At least, that's how Claire interpreted it.

On the night and early morning in question, he had actually seen the suspect twice. Around 9 PM, he had been at a rest area teaching a family about techniques used by the government to cover up the existence of Bigfoot and other cryptids. The children, he assured Kiko, had been fascinated, and had even seen Bigfoot themselves once or twice. He was, after all, known to roam around the Pacific Northwest.

At the rest area, Jackson had heard the familiar sounds of Bruce Springsteen's *Nebraska* album coming from a car parked near the van where the family lived. It was one of his favorite albums, he said, so he had wandered over to speak with the woman in the car.

He described her as mid to late sixties with sandy blonde hair. He'd asked her whether she knew that in 1984 Bruce Springsteen had been flipped by the CIA and had been a covert agent ever since. The woman had frowned and rolled up the window.

But for the next few hours, while educating the children about Chupacabra, he watched the woman out of the corner of his eye. He was fairly sure that she, too, was an undercover federal agent. The whole time she just watched each and every person as they came and went from the rest area. Didn't look at her phone, didn't look down once.

Jackson had lost track of her for a while, but later that night, around 11 PM, the rest area had mostly cleared out. He noticed that she was still there when he saw her get out of her car and head to the restroom. When she emerged she was accompanied by Barbara Stanwich, the sex worker who had later been found murdered.

Jackson didn't make much of this at first; after all, it wouldn't be the first time he'd seen an older woman pick up an older prostitute. But when he heard about her murder, he'd known the truth. Barbara Stanwich knew too much and had to be eliminated.

∼

Back at the car, Claire said, "Kiko, I'm beginning to think you are either the single most gifted actor of your generation, or a sociopath. How else could you become anyone and lie about anything on command?"

Kiko grinned. "Can't I be both?"

"Gimme the executive summary," Jack said.

"I don't believe this is a copycat at all," Claire said. "I think whoever this was has been involved from the beginning."

"How does the age timeline line up?" Jack asked.

"Can't you do the math?" Kiko asked.

Jack wiped sweat off his bald head. "It's hot as hell out here, and the fumes from the cars don't help. Let's say the woman is in her mid-sixties. The first murder was in 1979, forty-five years ago. That would put her at around twenty. It's definitely possible, and it might explain why people saw both a man and a woman in that sedan."

"That might leave Sanchez in the clear," Kiko said.

"My bet is that Cunningham somehow held sway over this woman, this young woman, at the time."

Claire was about to fill Jack in on the conversation when his phone rang. "Violet," he said. He tapped it, putting it on speakerphone. "Violet, you're on speakerphone with Kiko and Claire here. We just finished the interview."

"Get back here fast," Violet said. "Fitz has been attacked. Again."

CHAPTER THIRTY-THREE

FITZ GROANED in pain and tried to push Cunningham off of him. The man was old and frail, but he had enough strength left in his jaw to keep the grip tight on Fitz's ear. So, as he tried to push him off and Cunningham didn't let go of the ear, Fitz was forced to roll forward with him.

As he did, he fell to the floor, striking his head on the corner of Cunningham's bed frame. He came down on his side just as Cunningham released his bite.

Cunningham landed on him, then rolled off to the side.

Fitz could feel blood pooling into his ear canal from the bite. His head throbbed in pain. Out of the corner of his eye, he looked at Cunningham, who was now lying on his back on the floor. He was motionless, but Fitz knew he was alive because he was mumbling, "Taylor, Taylor, Taylor the gator. I'll come home, and then I'll save her. Taylor, Taylor the gator."

The fight was over, and Fitz, despite everything, found himself laughing.

He wasn't the kind of guy who sought out physical pain, but every time he experienced it, it actually made him feel better. He'd spent a good portion of his life numbing himself with pills and alcohol. In fact, Fitz considered himself a world-class expert at avoiding his feelings altogether.

Now, he reached up and touched the blood streaming from his ear. He counted the beats of the throbbing pain in his temple. He laughed at the physical pain because he was acutely aware of the deeper, stronger pain he was experiencing.

He thought back to when he and Claire had reconnected recently when he'd been brought in to work the case of the Color Killer. She'd been wearing a cream-colored pantsuit in the lobby of the Seattle FBI office. She was drinking a cappuccino and making fun of him. He'd railed against her for trying to live a neat and perfect life. He'd argued for the virtues of a messy, stumbling, bumbling, chaotic, drunken existence.

He had to hand it to himself, at least he was practicing what he preached.

Dr. Thacker appeared over him, looking down, his mouth moving. But all Fitz heard were stern mumblings.

He was in his own world. A world full of pain. A world full of hatred for Thacker's good looks and respectability. Hatred that the man had met Claire once and essentially declared his love. Fitz had worked with her for years and lied to himself about his own feelings damn near every moment.

Two male orderlies lifted Cunningham up and placed him back in his chair. Thacker hurried over and began attending to him.

Fitz sat up and held his hand up to his ear. The bottom of it was frayed, like a little flap of chicken skin hanging off the meat.

And still, all Fitz could do was laugh.

He loved to argue for the virtues of a chaotic, real, and messy life. And things were about to get messier than ever.

CHAPTER THIRTY-FOUR

AS THE HELICOPTER blades began to churn, creating a rhythm that vibrated through the air, Claire settled into her seat, feeling the gentle lift as the chopper ascended. Below her, the outskirts of Portland gradually shrank into a detailed miniature. The warmth of the sun seeped through the helicopter's windows, tempering the coolness of the air-conditioned interior, yet the day's mugginess seemed to linger as a faint sheen on her skin.

The city's grid began to give way to the lush, verdant sprawl of the Willamette Valley. From this height, the rivers appeared as glistening ribbons, their paths reflecting the bright sunlight. The Willamette itself stretched out below, its surface dotted with the tiny wakes of boats that looked more like water skimming insects from above.

They passed over small farms that checkerboarded the landscape, each plot a patchwork of various shades of green, where rows of vineyards aligned with precision, bordered by darker hedges. Occasionally, the uniformity was broken by a burst of color—fields of blooming flowers probably destined for local markets.

When they'd heard Fitz was injured, Jack had pulled every string he could to get them a helicopter back to Seattle, and Claire had agreed to deal with the consequences. There was no way in hell they were taking the three hours to drive back.

Jack had patched Claire's cell phone into her headset, and she dialed Violet, who sounded more ruffled than Claire had ever heard her. Her usual tone was fairly disinterested unless she happened to be talking about some aspect of technology. Now, she sounded genuinely concerned.

"He's lost a small part of his ear," Violet said, "and he may have a bit of a concussion, not to mention some blood loss."

Claire grimaced. "Cunningham did all that?"

"Details are still sketchy," Violet said. "He took his earpiece out so I couldn't hear everything. I'm at the facility now, and Fitz was just taken away to—"

"Don't let them take him out of the facility."

"No, they're treating him here. It's not *that* serious. But apparently, he hit his head on the corner of a metal bed frame or something. He fell off a chair. I don't know all the details."

"Is someone writing up a report?"

No response.

"Violet?"

The call had dropped, which Jack had warned her was likely.

Claire was concerned, but more than that, she was frustrated. She never should have let Fitz go there by himself. The man was a loose cannon. With Fitz she never knew whether he was more interested in getting to the truth or getting a rise out of a witness or suspect. And without her there as a mediating force, he'd probably said something or done something to provoke Cunningham.

As they moved further from the city, the terrain grew more rugged, hills rolling like waves frozen in time. Each hill cast long shadows in the low-angle sunlight, the undulations revealing hidden valleys and secluded ponds that mirrored the sky. The occasional cluster of cattle grazed on the hillsides, casting elongated shadows stretching lazily across the grass.

Further on, the landscape transformed again as they passed over a large state park. The dense forests below were a stark contrast to the open fields they'd just flown over. The trees stood densely packed, a deep, almost black green, interspersed with the occasional splash of a clearing or a sunlit glade.

Jack's voice came through her headset. "Try again now. Back in range, I think."

Claire called Violet again and launched right into it. "Here's what I want you to do. First, make sure Cunningham is held securely."

"Already on that," Violet replied. "The director prescribed some anxiolytics and the nurse has already given him the meds. They're saying he'll probably sleep for an hour or two. And we've got the local officer back on the door."

"Now," she said, "get back to the office. I'm pretty sure we're looking for an accomplice. A woman in her mid to late sixties."

"Taylor," Violet said. "Based on what Cunningham said, it's Taylor."

"I know Cunningham doesn't have any siblings, but I need you to look into every aspect of his past and see what you might find. Maybe the mascot thing, maybe someone he was close with... anything."

"Working on that," Violet said, "As they took Fitz away on the stretcher, he said that Cunningham was saying something about 'Taylor the gator,' and then something about a cousin and about 'saving her.'"

"Pull every record of who played the role of the school mascot, if they even have records for that. They probably don't, but maybe you can get someone on the phone, some old-timer who is still around, or some school principal. If there are any court records or birth records or anything digitized from that area of Louisiana in the forties, fifties, and sixties, look for any family connection, anyone at all."

"What are you gonna do?" Violet asked.

"Jack's looking for a place to land this thing as close as possible to the facility. I'm going to get Gus to tell me the real name of his accomplice. I just have to figure out how."

CHAPTER THIRTY-FIVE

JACK HAD BEEN able to arrange a landing spot on the helipad at the local precinct of the Seattle PD. Since they had left their SUV back in Portland, they were now down to zero cars. Thankfully, Jack had a solution for that as well. He'd had Kathy, Hightower's assistant, order a car service, assuring her that he would cover the cost himself. Claire knew that a confrontation with Jonathan and Hightower was coming anyway, so why not add another fifty bucks to the tab?

The memory care facility was only ten minutes from the precinct, and by the time they got there, Claire had a plan. But as she rushed into the lobby, her plan evaporated immediately.

She was greeted by two security guards and Thacker, who was not smiling as much as the last time he had seen her. She hadn't responded to his flurry of texts, and she wasn't sure if he was more upset about that or about the fact that, for a second time, Fitz had provoked one of his patients into violence. She hoped he could keep it professional, but that hope quickly vanished.

"Agent Anderson," he said flatly. "I thought you might not still be alive."

Claire studied his face and saw that he'd taken her silence personally. "Where is Fitz Pembroke?" she asked.

"He is being attended to." He nodded down the hallway to his right. "He's fine. I can't say as much for my patient though."

"I need to ask Cunningham some questions," Claire said.

He scoffed. "Absolutely not. Not only is he sedated, but your team has upset him to the point that I'm worried for his life. Falling can be a sentinel event for a man of that age."

"My understanding is that he didn't fall. He lunged at a federal agent."

"Be that as it may," Thacker said, "you can't interview a sleeping man."

Claire stepped back. "What are these guys for?" She indicated the two security guards.

"We've cooperated up to this point," Thacker said, "but if you want to speak with any of my patients again, you will need a court order. And I *will* fight it. No matter what he's done in the past, I cannot have one of my patients battered by the FBI. Your team is reckless and *dishonest*."

Jack, who'd been holding himself back, was not having it. "You know we will get any court order we want, right? If these two bozos are supposed to intimidate us..." he trailed off, shaking his head.

Thacker frowned. "Be that as it may—"

"Just speak normally for God's sake." Claire was growing irritated at his overuse of the expression.

He smirked. "*Be that as it may*, the court order *will* be necessary."

With that, he turned and walked away, shoving his

hands in his pockets and strolling down the hall as though he had not a worry in the world.

"Let's go check on Fitz," Claire said.

They found him in surprisingly good spirits. The side of his head had been bandaged, as had his ear, and he was sipping a bottle of Coca-Cola from a straw. "Awww," he declared as they walked in. "You *came*. I didn't know you cared."

The medical room was a compact space painted in a soothing sage green. A sturdy oak cabinet with glass-paneled doors lined one wall and was neatly stocked with gauze, bandages, and medications. A small window allowed a sliver of natural light to filter in, casting a thin beam across the speckled linoleum floor, adding a touch of warmth to the otherwise utilitarian space.

"How are you feeling?" Claire asked.

"Maria here gave me her Coke," Fitz said, nodding toward a young nurse sitting in the corner.

"What did you do, Fitz?" Claire asked.

"I guess you could say I provoked him."

"I mean, I'm not surprised you provoked him again. But why do it so close to his proximity a second time? You knew the man was capable of drawing blood, did you think something different would happen this time?"

"That's the thing with me," Fitz said. "I'm incapable of growth."

Claire sighed heavily.

Her parents weren't there for her growing up because they couldn't be. Fitz's parents had been absent by choice. And while Claire's uncle taught her she only needed to keep continuing to grow, across the pond Fitz was being raised by nannies whose sole responsibility was to keep him fed and quiet. He'd grown up hoping to garner attention from his parents, but they had only shown the slightest interest when they could use his above-average intelligence as a party trick. Both Claire and Fitz were focused internally, but Fitz desperately craved external validation.

Claire sat on a little plastic chair next to him. His beard was wilder than ever, but something in his face looked childlike as he sipped the soda from the straw.

"We know it's a woman in her mid-sixties," Claire said. "Apparently she's a fan of early Bruce Springsteen and murdering redheaded prostitutes. We figure she would have been around twenty at the time of the first killing. That ring any bells?"

Fitz considered this. "That's good detail. No doubt this is Taylor, but I wouldn't have guessed she was that young. Although I guess it's not a shock."

"What does her age matter?" Claire asked.

"You'll have to ask Kiko. She's the one who likes to do the math on that sort of thing."

"What sort of thing?" Claire asked.

"On what is an acceptable age gap in a romantic relationship." Fitz shook his head and looked at Claire in a way she didn't quite understand. "You know, Agent Anderson, this whole thing has been a love story all along."

CHAPTER THIRTY-SIX

AN HOUR LATER, they were back in the Boiler Room, gathered around their usual table. They needed to eat, but Claire hadn't wanted to allow time for a break. Instead, she'd asked Kathy to send down the leftover muffins and pastries from a meeting that had happened earlier in the day.

Now, the whole crew munched on sad, stale muffins and drank cold coffee out of styrofoam cups. No one was sharing pastries with Ranger, so he lay on the floor next to his bed, periodically looking into a team member's eyes and letting out a pitiful moan or an exaggerated yawn.

Violet wanted the team to weigh in on new information that she promised would break the case wide open. Sitting at her usual station of computers along the wall, she tapped a button and the large screen lit up.

Claire chewed on a dry scone as she watched a series of photos appear on the screen. The first showed a black-and-white photograph of a high school football field and a person dressed in a poorly designed alligator mascot costume standing in the foreground.

"I started with the mascot. I wasn't able to find anyone who knew Cunningham while he was in high school, but I was able to reach the current gym teacher," Violet said. "And I'm not making this up. He walked over to the school's trophy and memory case while I was on the phone with him. Apparently, the gator is a big deal down there. High school football is huge, and there's actually been competition for the role of the gator since the sixties. They have a list of everyone who has played the role over the last seventy-five years. I looked at the years 1949, which is the first year they tracked this, through the mid-sixties. Figuring that those are the years someone roughly matching the age range when the accomplice you believe exists would have been in high school."

The next images that passed across the screen were of a series of yearbook photos, the typical sorts of headshot portraits that many yearbooks used.

"Most of them were men, and I ruled them out," Violet continued. "It sounds like you have enough evidence to know this is a woman. Over the years, there were only three women who played that role; Eloise Broussard, Cecelia Fontenot, and Marie-Thérèse Landry."

Violet paused to let the team study the pictures of the women.

"The first of the three died two years ago. The second two are alive. Marie-Thérèse is still living in the same small town. I called and reached her husband, who said she was at a doctor's appointment and would be back later. He seemed to have no idea what I was talking about. It's Cecelia Fontenot who interests me the most. She would be sixty-seven years old now and acted as the school mascot between 1973 and 1974. By 1975, she must have left town because records of her ceased entirely. She pops up again in 1990 in California, when she changed her name to Cecelia

Butterman and had a child, born in Concord, California. He is now thirty-four years old and still living in the Bay Area. Michael Butterman."

"Any connection between Cecelia and Gus Cunningham?" Claire asked.

"I'll wager a chunk of my intact ear that they were lovers," Fitz said.

"I looked into Cecelia's mother, and she died right around the time Cecelia left town."

"Died under what circumstances?" Kiko asked.

"Well, there's actually no record of her death. She is presumed dead. She simply disappeared," Violet said.

Jack frowned. "That's suspicious."

"Not exactly," Violet said, "She could have hit the road for California with her daughter. The records are unclear. There's more to look into there. But I want to show you all this."

She tapped her keyboard one more time and a new photo came up. This one was from a trade magazine article about the opening of a series of Sunny Skillet diners in Northern California.

It was a photo of Augustus Cunningham standing out front of a diner holding a large pair of scissors. It must have been a ribbon cutting ceremony and he looked every bit the cheesy regional manager—neon pink, yellow, and blue geometric designs splattered across a black silk tie. Violet zoomed in on the picture, which showed a young woman wearing a pink button-front dress with thick shoulder pads, maybe in her late twenties, standing off to the side. "I believe this is Cecelia Fontenot, before she changed her name."

Claire noticed that her hands were clasped below a slightly protruding belly. "When is the photo from?"

"1989," Violet said. "Right around the time of the final

murder. Assuming she is a few months pregnant here—four or five—the timeline works with the birth of Michael Butterman."

"Lovers, just as I expected," Fitz said. "But I was not thinking there was a child involved."

There was a knock at the door, the knock Claire had been dreading.

It opened a crack, and Claire saw the usually friendly face of Gerald Hightower. "We need to talk," he said in a neutral tone that someone might mistake for cordial. His face was anything but friendly.

"Everyone?" Claire asked.

"No, Claire," he said solemnly. "Just you."

CHAPTER THIRTY-SEVEN

"FITZ IS OFF THE CASE," Hightower stated, "and we may not be able to use him as a consultant anymore."

Claire was expecting an admonishment, but not this. She sat across from Hightower, his desk gleaming under the light, and closed her eyes softly while taking a long inhale.

"Look," he continued, "this isn't coming from me, but it *is* coming from me. I mean, I don't have a choice in the matter."

"I see," Claire said.

"It's already legally dicey to use consultants like Fitz; now he might have a concussion, and there are liability issues with the facility. Evergreen." He glanced at a stack of papers on his desk as though they were the sword of Damocles hanging over him. He let out a long, thin stream of air. "Now that we're in this mess, I feel like I shouldn't have talked you out of retiring."

"You didn't sway my decision to stay," Claire said. "I say what I want and make my own decisions."

"Anyway," Hightower continued. "We need to sacrifice a

limb to save the body. What do you need from the agency to sever Fitz as quietly and painlessly as possible and get this case closed quickly?"

"I need you to stall," Claire said. "Don't take Fitz off the case until after we solve it."

"Do we at least have a smoking gun?"

"We are close. Violet has a name, a birth name, and a description of our suspect. Our *second* suspect. She can use her AI photo tools to produce an aged-up version. We'll get it out to law enforcement throughout the Pacific Northwest. And we already know it matches a description that we received from an eyewitness this morning in Portland."

"That's another thing I needed to speak with you about."

"The helicopter?" Claire asked.

Hightower shook his head. "Not that, although Jonathan has already assured me he is writing up a report about it. Is there any chance you made up a special unit? A Joint Task Force that serves as a communication link between the FBI, the CIA, NASA, the Secret Service, and an as yet undisclosed intergalactic confederacy?"

"How did you find that out?"

"Kathy had a call forwarded to her from the tip line. Apparently, a guy named America Jackson has inside information on Kiko. He never would have gotten through if he hadn't known her full name. Apparently, he has evidence proving she is actually one of the lizard aliens wearing a human skin suit and has infiltrated this secret task force with the intent to inflict mind control on the homeless population of Portland en masse."

He closed his eyes as though the ridiculousness of this genuinely pained him.

"What we did got us our suspect," Claire said defiantly.

"I don't know what will happen when this case is over,"

he said, "but I know we have a killer out there who is still an immediate, lethal threat and one at Evergreen capable of committing murder one bite at a time. Look, Fitz is off this case and there's nothing I can do about that. But you can still bring this home before someone else is killed."

When Claire returned to the office, Jack and Kiko were already gone. She gave a sigh of relief that Fitz had left as well. If she couldn't find him, she couldn't fire him.

Violet sat alone at the large table, which was unusual for her as she rarely ventured more than a few feet from her computers. She wore a baggy sweatshirt with faded lettering that read MIT, the university from which she'd been expelled. She was munching on Lay's potato chips, offering Ranger every fourth chip as she methodically worked her way through the bag.

Claire sat across from her.

Violet noticed her staring, "What's up boss?"

"Dogs aren't supposed to have too much people food," Claire said. "That's a lot of salt for a pup."

"I only gave him one or two," Violet said. She looked down at Ranger as she brought her index finger to her lips in a whisper gesture, then winked at him before giving him another chip.

"Where are Jack and Kiko?" Claire asked, worried about how Violet would respond.

"They went out to pick up dinner. Pizza. We're all crashing from the pastries, and they've decided what we need is more pastries smothered in a thick layer of dairy. If they bring back something with onions, I'm going to blow a fuse."

Claire had known she'd have to have a conversation with

Violet eventually, and this seemed like as good an opportunity as any. She stood up and closed the door, then sat back down.

"You and Kiko," she began, "you two alright?"

"Fine," Violet said.

"Come on," Claire said, "I've known Kiko longer than I've known you, but I think I know you a little bit. Initially, when I decided to take on the role of leading this task force, I knew there could be an issue with a love triangle. Is that what's going on here?"

Violet laughed, but Claire detected a hint of bitterness.

"Not at all," Violet said. "No." When Claire didn't say anything, Violet continued. "Jack and I had two dates before we began working together. The day he walked in and I knew we were going to be on the same task force, I told him it was over. I figured those were the rules in a place like this. Anyway, I wasn't going to jeopardize the ticket out of jail this job had offered me by continuing to date him."

Claire felt a twinge of guilt. Perhaps she should have ordered Kiko and Jack not to see each other outside of work at her first inkling of their budding relationship.

"Aren't those the rules?" Violet asked.

Claire sighed. "Yes, they are. And it's my job to speak with them."

"I'm not saying you should have." Violet crunched up her empty bag and tossed it toward the corner, but it caught air as it expanded and landed a few feet short.

Ranger meandered over and began sniffing inside the bag. It got caught on his nose and he shook his head to free himself.

Violet chuckled. "The way I see it, rules are made to be considered. And, what about your own workplace relationship?"

Claire was genuinely confused. "You mean Thacker? No way. He sent me a series of unrequited texts that were on the verge of begging me to go out with him. I'm not so sure I've heard the last from him. But I'm hoping I have."

"No," Violet said. "I wasn't talking about *him.*"

Claire shrugged.

"Fitzgerald Pembroke III."

"Are you serious?" Claire was baffled. "We've worked together for quite a few years, and no, there has never been anything between us, and never would be. You see the way he talks to me. He hates me."

Violet drummed her fingers on the table. "Remember what a crush looked like in grade school?"

"Yes, but Fitz and I are *adults,*" Claire said.

"You really don't see it, do you?"

"See what?" Claire asked.

"Emotionally, Fitz is still at the level of a fourteen year old. And, he's in love with you."

Claire was about to object, but the look of resigned knowing in Violet's eyes kept her silent.

A hundred interactions with Fitz raced through her mind. He had never once made any attempt at anything romantic with her. And though he said inappropriate things all the time, none indicated any romantic interest. But the more her mind objected, the more her gut was becoming convinced that Violet was right. The timing made sense. Maybe her divorce going final had shifted something in him.

"Did he tell you that himself?" Claire asked.

Violet shook her head. "No, but I figured it out during his interview with Cunningham. The timbre of his voice told me he was going madder and madder, and the way he cracked when they got on the subject of love made everything come together." She lowered her voice. "I've seen the way he looks at you when he doesn't think you'll notice. *And* he's been trying to wear nicer clothes lately. At least for him."

Claire *had* noticed his new blue suit. She pressed her hands into the table. "I can't do this right now. I need to get a coffee and focus on the case."

"I'm heading out, too," Violet said. "I don't want to be here when Jack and Kiko return."

"Even if you're mad that Jack has chosen to date Kiko, you need to find a way through those feelings," Claire said. "We need this team to work together."

"I'm not mad that Kiko is dating Jack," Violet said. "If you're going to let romances happen, I do *not* care in the least. Kiko and Jack can date whoever they want, same as I do."

"Then what is it?" Claire asked. "Why do you and Kiko get into these little spats?"

"Ugh," Violet groaned. "This is going to make me sound like a total black hole, but it's Kiko's positive can-do attitude that rubs me the wrong way. Dancing and flirting and being out there and positive. Like, doesn't she know how terrible everything is?"

Before Claire could even respond, Violet grabbed her backpack and scurried out.

Claire looked around the empty room, exhaustion spreading over her. Their little task force had barely lasted two months, and now it was in disarray.

Fitz was supposed to be off the case, and God knew where he was.

Violet, the smartest person on the team, was alienated from the rest of them for what seemed like a petty emotional reaction. The only two people who were happy were Kiko and Jack, and, according to the rules, Claire was going to have to put an end to that.

She had no chance of holding this little unit together.
FBI task force S.W.O.R.D. had failed.
She had failed.

PART 3

PARADISE ON THE SALISH SEA

CHAPTER THIRTY-EIGHT

CLAIRE HAD TOLD everyone to arrive by 7 AM, but as she strolled down the hall holding her cappuccino, it was only six fifteen.

She needed this time alone in the office to think about how to handle the day, the case, and her team. She needed to tell Jack and Kiko that they had to end things unless one of them left the squad. She had already decided not to treat Fitz any differently. She wasn't sure if Violet was right about him, and it didn't make any sense to bring it up.

She had sent him a text telling him not to come in, but to stay by his phone. She didn't tell him that he was suspended, or that he was off the case. Rather, she'd explained that since they filed an actual report for his earlobe injury, he was medically required to stay out for the time being, and she was working on it.

She stopped a couple of yards from the door, which, oddly, was closed. She heard music, which didn't make any sense. She moved closer and held her ear up to the door. Typically, the cleaning crew dealt with the room after hours and left the door propped open.

Now she was fairly sure she was hearing Pearl Jam's song *Black* playing incredibly loudly, loud enough that it was too loud for her, and she had a wall separating her ear from the source of the sound. She cracked the door and was consumed by the smell of stale beer.

"Oh no," she whispered.

Fitz lay on his back on the floor under the wall-mounted monitor. There were three empty beer cans around him, but she was fairly sure he'd had more than that.

The song reached its climax, Eddie Vedder nearly screaming the final words.

I know you'll be a star, in somebody else's sky
But why, why, why can't it be
Oh, can't it be mine?

As Claire watched him, the song ended, then began again. Fitz had it on repeat.

"Fitz, get up."

"Ah, yes," he said. "My Beatrice is here."

His words weren't slurred, making her think he might have had his last beer a few hours ago. Not that it helped. He was still a mess.

"Do you know," he said, sitting up, "why most people read *The Inferno,* but not the other books of *The Divine Comedy?*"

Claire sipped her cappuccino for dear life. "Why?" she asked.

"Because, let's be honest, most of us don't think we'll get into heaven. And, when we look into the abyss of our own evil, we don't want to move past it. You know why?"

"I don't," Claire said as she picked up the empty beer cans and set them in the trash. "I don't know why."

Using a chair to push himself up, he slowly rose. "Because we don't want to do the work it will take to make ourselves change. We don't want to look past our own navels to make the world a better place." Fitz laughed loudly. "If we can't be in heaven, we'd rather burn in hell. I know, I know, I've made myself unfit for permanent companionship."

"Fitz, you need to get out of here," Claire said. "You got my text. You know you're not supposed to be here."

"Ask me?" he said, ignoring her, "I think of the three, *Purgatorio* is the most important for us to read." He laughed bitterly. "If you're in hell, it's easy, you just lie there and suffer. In Heaven, even if your celestial realm isn't close enough to share a pint with God, you're still in paradise, right? Purgatory is *life*. It's where the real stuff happens. It's where we truly get to understand what it means to be human. Yes. Purgatory is where the waltz takes place."

Fitz stumbled and fell against the wall with a loud thud. Claire hurried over and helped him up. She was pissed as hell, but she just needed to get him out of the building.

Fitz looked over at Ranger, who was sleeping in the corner, seemingly oblivious to his best friend's mental state.

"Here boy," Fitz called. "Ranger, you want treats? Here boy."

"I will take care of Ranger," Claire said. "Fitz, you need to leave."

"*And thence we came forth to see again the stars.*" He repeated the line in Italian. "*E quindi uscimmo a riveder le stelle.*"

Claire watched Fitz's stumbling walk become a sloppy dance as he walked out, singing to the tune of *Waltzing Matilda*:

Waltzing through Purgatory
Waltzing through Purgatory
And his ghost may be heard as it sings for his Beatrice
Who'll come a'waltzing through purgatory with me?

Half an hour later, Claire heard voices in the hall.

Before she could take a deep breath, Violet and Kiko burst through the door and she braced herself for the confrontation, figuring they were finally having it out and she'd have to mediate.

But the exact opposite was true.

Kiko bounded up with a wide smile. "Violet took me out last night."

"Umm, okay, that seems like it went well?" Claire asked, looking over at Violet.

Violet nodded.

"Claire, don't worry about the me and Jack thing. It is squashed," Kiko said. "I want to apologize to the team for breaking the rules. We talked it all out and got over our differences and whatever."

Violet was nodding along, not quite as enthusiastically as Kiko. But Violet had never been as enthusiastic as Kiko about anything before in her life.

"And there's something else," Violet said, hurrying over to her computer. "Late last night and into this morning, we may have cracked this thing wide open. Again."

Ranger glanced up, probably because of the vibration in the floor, then went back to sleep. He hadn't seen or smelled any food and he enjoyed sleeping more than anything short of a treat.

Violet sat at her monitor, and the screen lit up. As it did, Jack entered, and Claire couldn't read anything on his face. But she knew he was professional enough to lock into work when the time came.

"We were able to get some genealogical records from Cunningham's hometown. We already knew that both of his parents had died in a car crash before he'd gone to live with his aunt. In the records we had, his aunt's name was Mary LaGrange. We couldn't find much about her, only that she had passed away when he was in his late thirties, long after he had moved away."

"What we found last night was that Mary LaGrange changed her name to Gretchen Fontenot. That is, Gretchen was her middle name, and she got married to a man named Simon Fontenot. They divorced soon after, but she kept his name."

Claire was putting it all together in her head. "So, Augustus Cunningham was raised by his aunt, Mary LaGrange, aka Gretchen Fontenot, who is also the mother of Cecelia Fontenot, aka *Taylor*."

"Holy hell," Jack exclaimed.

"Exactly," Kiko agreed.

"I couldn't have said it better myself," Violet added.

Violet had stood and was now facing the whole team. She brushed her black hair away from her face and adjusted her glasses.

"I got a woman on the phone who keeps the records for the town. Dottie is her name, and she must be at least eighty-five years old. A nice lady, the kind who knows every piece of gossip in town," Violet explained. "She said that Gretchen Fontenot disappeared right around the same time that Cecelia moved out of town. And the odd thing was that they left their little farmhouse abandoned. Cute little property with a lovely little pond and the fattest frogs in Louisiana, she told me. Didn't try to sell it, nothing. Gretchen Fontenot just fell off the face of the earth."

"What about a father?" Claire asked.

"No father on the birth certificate," Violet said. "Could have been a one night thing, or even—and I hate to say it—rape. We may never know who Cecelia's father was. But there's one more thing. Dottie said that paperwork showed up at the courthouse a few years later, in the late seventies, showing that Cecelia was, in fact, adopted."

Claire paced the room. "That makes no sense. She had a birth certificate, with a hospital and everything on it, right?"

"It was a home birth," Violet said.

"Okay, but later, paperwork arrived that showed she'd been adopted?"

"The way Dottie explained it to me, the paperwork was from a law firm representing Cecelia Fontenot. Something about establishing residency in Canada or something. She'd learned through genealogy and DNA that her real mother was Canadian, and her 'mother' had adopted her, then faked the birth certificate."

"That makes very little sense," Jack said.

Claire nodded. "But maybe it doesn't need to."

"So," Kiko said, "are we thinking that Augustus Cunningham and Cecelia Fontenot ran off together?"

"Yes," Violet said, "right after the disappearance of Gretchen, who was both Cecelia's mother and Augustus's aunt. Most likely, they killed Gretchen on the way out the door. By the way," she added, "Gretchen was a redhead. Went to the same beauty parlor as my new friend Dottie."

"I'm glad he's not here to witness me saying this," Jack said, "but I think Fitz was right all along. At its center, this whole case has been a love story."

CHAPTER THIRTY-NINE

ONE MORE WOULD END THIS, I had told myself. One more would be enough. But it wasn't.

Now I drive up and down this cursed interstate, stopping at rest areas, at diners, looking for her, looking for mother.

It had been over thirty years since the last time. It had been so long, and in that time, I had raised a son. My son.

When I left, after the woman in Yreka, I thought I would start a new life that would last forever. I never called him, never wrote him, never even sent him a postcard. I started my new life and, in many ways, it was a *good* one.

My son. My son is good.

He's the only one who is.

In the past I convinced myself I was good. I had a scapegoat. Nothing was my fault. But now I know how evil I am. I'm just like my mother.

Worse, maybe.

At least she never killed anyone. She was never the crane.

The rest area is empty save for a fat man in a little car

and young mom with a mean-looking husband and an armful of babies. The next off ramp has a diner, a Sunny Skillet, one of the ones we opened.

That day when Gus finally killed her, it felt so wrong and so right. And as we drove away, out of Louisiana and through the South and eventually up into California, I simply forgot about her.

And for years Gus and I lived almost like brother and sister. We were cousins, but closer than that. And Gus never once tried anything then, though sometimes I got the feeling that he wanted to.

When we learned that I'd been adopted, everything changed.

I resisted at first, couldn't believe it, but Gus was sure, and he had the adoption paperwork to prove it.

I think I *wanted* to believe it. By then, I didn't know any better. I didn't have the urges he had, but when we first made love, it was nice.

And when, soon after, we visited Bellingham, and we saw that woman, everything felt right then, too. I felt a sense of peace and relief watching Gus. After he did it, after he sat her up and made her look at the water forever, we made love right there on the beach before we drove South on I-5.

In Bellingham was the first, the woman in Yreka was the last.

Then, when I knew I had a baby in me, things changed. I left. I thought it was over.

Until a couple days ago.

Sometimes I think that even though we aren't related by blood, what we did was wrong.

Not the killing. Those women deserved it.

Gus and I never should have coupled. But then I wouldn't have my son. And my son is good.

I arrive.

The diner has been updated, but the menu is largely the same. "I'll have the coffee and the Sausage Skillet Sunny Side."

There's no one here, no fat little froggies, no one enough like mother.

I look up. At least there's TV.

One more. Maybe the right woman will come into the diner.

And she will be the last.

CHAPTER FORTY

SOMETHING WAS BUGGING CLAIRE, but she wasn't entirely sure what. She had heard of many cases in which people found out they were adopted later in life after having been raised as a biological child. It wasn't super common, but it was far from unheard of. "Violet," she called across the room, "did you share all this with Fitz?"

"Yes, he's working on it from home." Claire put her cell on speakerphone and dialed.

"Fitz Pembroke," he answered.

"I'm glad you made it home, Fitz," Claire said.

His heavy breathing made Claire think he'd hurried across the room to grab the phone. Whatever she could say about him, she knew he wanted to do the job and would feel even worse having been removed from the office.

"I'm going to ask you some questions," Claire said. "Jack, Kiko, and Violet are all here and listening in. This adoption thing, how can you explain it?"

"Yes, that," Fitz began. "I put myself in the mind of Augustus Cunningham, raised by what I'm assuming was a truly wicked aunt. It's difficult to discern because of his deteriorating mental state, but I believe we were seeing signs of horrific trauma and possibly even torture reflected in some of his behavior."

"Right," Claire said.

"But he made it out," Fitz continued, "he left the little town. One day he comes back, and there is a girl there, twenty-something years younger than him. His aunt had raised him starting when she was so young, now she's in her early forties and has a baby. And he sees this woman torturing this innocent little baby like he had been tortured. And I don't mean she was tortured like ice picks under the fingernails, but psychological torture, probably beatings, cruelty every single day, you can fill in the details. I believe he felt for this girl. In my interview with him, he mentioned that he had saved Taylor, his nickname for her because she had played Taylor the Gator. I believe they killed her together and took off across the country. Then, their second murder, the one in Bellingham, which one might consider counting as their first, was only one year after the paperwork showed up saying that she was adopted."

"You think he forged the paperwork?" Claire asked.

"I do," Fitz answered. "I think he was in love with his cousin. It didn't matter to him that they were related. Something in his twisted moral code allowed him to convince his little Taylor that she was adopted. He hoped that would be enough to convince her to change the way she felt about him, and I guess it was."

Claire drummed her fingers on the table. "That is deeply sick."

"And that's one of the least sick things yet." Fitz let out a long breath. "I believe that when they started having sex, the act triggered a mutual craziness—a *folie à deux*—which led to our string of serial killings. If the photo Violet sent me is truly Cecelia Fontenot, at some point she got pregnant. And knowing she couldn't bring a child into the scene the way things were, she split and the killing stopped. My hunch is that her absence was enough to break the murderous spell. Gus Cunningham started his spree soon after they became intimate, and stopped when she disappeared from his life."

Claire thought for a long time, then said, "I have an idea. Ever heard of the saying 'Hell hath no fury like a woman's scorn'?"

"The actual quote," Fitz said, "is 'Hell has no fury like a woman scorned.' There is an important distinction to be made that..." Fitz stopped himself. "Close enough."

"Thanks for all your help Fitz," Claire said. "We'll talk soon."

She ended the call.

"What are you going to do?" Jack asked.

Thankfully, he had let Fitz have his moment and remained silent during the call.

"Well, you know how much I hate going on television." Claire stood. "I'm going to do just that. And you three are coming with me."

She had called the press conference for a little after noon. Interest in the case had exploded, so every television station in the city was there, plus representatives from all the national cable news networks. The local papers had also sent reporters.

Claire stood at the lectern with Jack on her left, Violet and Kiko on her right. "I am Agent Claire Anderson, and this is my team, FBI Task Force S.W.O.R.D. As you may know, we have been working on a cold case that recently got hot: the case of the Interstate Reaper."

She nodded at Kiko, who held up a large printout that showed both Augustus Cunningham and Cecelia Fontenot.

"These are our killers," Kiko said, leaning into the microphone. "The first is in custody at Evergreen Memory Care, but the second is not. If anyone has information on the whereabouts of Cecelia Fontenot, please call the number you see on your screen, or printed on any reputable website that has hosted this video."

Kiko stepped back and Claire continued. "We believe that Miss Fontenot was an unwitting accomplice to the past murders, but may now be fully involved. We also believe that she was lied to by her cousin, Augustus Cunningham. We believe he fabricated evidence that she was adopted in order to betray and form an incestuous relationship with her." Claire gestured to her right. "Allow me to introduce Vivian Greene and Violet Wei, both experts in genealogy and research."

Of course, neither Kiko nor Violet had any such expertise, but this performance was for Cecelia Fontenot, and Claire needed to sell a story that would hook her.

"To my left," Claire continued, "is Jack Russo. He conducted a comprehensive interview with Augustus Cunningham, who admitted to fabricating the adoption paperwork. He's one of the finest psychological interrogators in the world." She almost smiled as she said it, knowing that Fitz would be watching. Right now he'd either be fuming or laughing hysterically. Possibly both.

"I'm sure I don't need to point out how devious, sick, and twisted this is. What's more is that we believe their relationship led to the string of killings that became known as the Interstate Reaper. Now," Claire concluded, "I'll be happy to take your questions."

Claire was certain Cecelia Fontenot would take action in response to this new information.

All Claire needed to do now was have her team ready when she did.

CHAPTER FORTY-ONE

A WARM RAIN had begun to fall as Claire sat in the driver's seat of the SUV, which she'd paid to be driven back from Portland out of her own pocket. Jack was to her right in the passenger seat and Kiko sat in the back.

"Tell me again," Jack said, "why aren't we just sitting in the lobby?"

"Two reasons," Claire replied. "First, they don't want us in their facility. After the second fight with Fitz, they got a temporary court order to allow local police to secure the door and to keep us out. We could get it overturned, but that would conflict with the second reason—I think it's actually better that we are out here."

"Why is that?" Kiko asked.

Claire glanced down at the eight-by-ten photo of Cecelia Fontenot. Violet had used an artificial intelligence program to appropriately age up the photo of her as a young pregnant woman. She had also used the program to create an image of what the son of Fontenot and Cunningham might look like at his current age.

"Because," Claire said, "if she shows up, I want to stop

her before she can even get in the facility. Speaking of which..." She pressed the button on the walkie-talkie that she'd been storing in the cup holder. "Mary, Hector, anything?"

Claire had stationed two junior agents by the door at the back of the facility. She didn't know them well, but Hightower had allowed her to borrow them from their usual counterterrorism assignment. She'd assured Hightower that Fontenot would show up once she learned that Cunningham had tricked her with the forged adoption paperwork. In truth, she wasn't certain that she would, but it was her best bet.

"I know it's against everything you stand for," Kiko said, "but I have an idea. You never replied to Stalker McSteamy, did you?"

"Can we not call Thacker that? Despite the fact that he was a bit aggressive or, well, creepy, we don't need to call him that."

"Fine," Kiko said dryly, "Creepy Nurse Guy, it is. Here's my point, even though the team is being shunned right now, he might have something to say about what's going on inside the facility. What is Cunningham up to? Is he cognizant? Did the facility get any strange calls? Has Cunningham received any personal calls? I don't know, maybe there's something he can tell us."

Claire tried to think of objections, but quickly realized that it wasn't a bad idea. Whipping her phone out of her purse, she sent Thacker a text.

Look, I'm sorry I didn't text you back. I really did enjoy meeting you and was flattered that you invited me out but I'm only recently divorced and you came on a little bit strong for what I'm used to. But I don't mean to reach out to you about this alone.

Almost immediately Claire got a response.

Please, go on.

"It's like he's been hovering over his phone waiting for you to text him," Kiko said. "Creepy."

Claire ignored her.

I'm reaching out both to tell you how sorry I am about the interactions between our psychological consultant and your patient. Also to warn you. And I don't say this to take anything away from how everything went down but we do know for certain that this patient is one of the most wanted serial killers in the country. We have reason to believe someone may wish to cause him harm. Within the restrictions that have been placed on our team, we have been watching your facility closely, for your own safety. But we do need your help. Has the facility received any strange calls or interactions today?

She let Kiko read the text over her shoulder.

Kiko gave her approval with a nod.

Claire pressed send and set her phone in the cup holder.

She stared out at the puddles forming in the parking lot. Back at her little waterfront house in Kingston, her paradise on the Salish Sea, she loved being out on the deck with a glass of wine. Even on days when it rained, and especially when it was warm, there was nothing she loved more than listening to the sound of the rain patter on the patio umbrella as she watched the beach get soaked and the millions of little droplets hit the water. She wished she was back there right now.

Her phone vibrated. Another text from Thacker. At least he had taken a beat to consider his response.

I do have information. Meet me at the side door. It's the delivery entrance for the kitchen. And don't worry, you won't need your umbrella, there's a little overhang so you won't be getting wet.

Claire read the text and then held it up to Kiko. "Since you're my relationship expert, what do you think this means?"

"Most likely that he actually has information and he

hopes this is a way into your pants," Kiko chuckled. "I'm sorry to say it so crassly, but..." she trailed off, shaking her head. "Men sometimes..."

"Men sometimes what?" Jack interjected with some heat in his voice.

"I don't know, you're probably right Jack, maybe I've just become jaded."

Claire thought for a moment, then said, "I'm going."

She hopped out of the car and jogged across the parking lot.

The rain had let up slightly, but she felt her hair dampen, and it felt good. She was aware of the roiling emotional aftermath of her marriage. The years they'd spent together would always be a part of her. But just like the rain could brighten a dull rock, perhaps the stormy ending of her marriage could make her more vibrant, too. And who knew? Maybe Thacker would turn out to be an amazing guy who just got a little tipsy and sent a couple of aggressive texts out of ignorance. If so, she could forgive him for that.

She walked around the side of the building and saw Thacker standing under the awning, looking handsome as ever.

"Thanks for meeting with me," Claire said. "I'm sorry that we've set up a stake out in your parking lot. But the situation is very serious."

"I know," he said.

Thacker stood towering over Claire and looking into her eyes expectantly.

The intensity of the rain swelled. Claire scooched in next to him under the awning to keep dry. The space was too small for them to stand more than twelve inches apart. She found it difficult to suppress the feeling that Thacker had known this.

"Do you have any information?" Claire finally asked, breaking the spell.

"I do," he said.

~

Jack stared out the window, watching around the corner for Claire to return. From the back seat, he heard Kiko's voice.

"We need to talk, Jack."

Jack glanced toward the entrance of the facility. "I don't like the sound of this. Did Claire find out?"

"Claire already knew," Kiko said, "but that's not what happened. I spoke with Violet."

"You know I was up front about her—and with her—from the beginning."

He could feel himself getting defensive. He didn't like being the bad guy. He'd never been in a serious, long-term relationship, but he'd never considered himself a player, either. He had met Violet before he'd known they'd be working together. They'd gone on a couple of dates, and honestly, he *did* find her attractive. Fitz would probably have some brilliant psychoanalysis explaining the deep recesses of his mind, but to him it was simple. Violet was different, and he liked that. They made out once, and then she broke it off the moment she learned they'd be working together.

But with Kiko it felt more serious. The mutual attraction had been immediate, the relationship had moved fast. But, judging by the tone of her voice, it was about to end.

"So what is it?" he asked.

"This is my first real assignment with the FBI. I'm lucky to have it, and I wouldn't have it without Claire. I only just got out from under my probationary period."

"And you're doing a good job," Jack said. "An excellent job."

"Wait, what is happening?" Kiko pointed toward the entrance.

Jack glanced out and read the side of the small passenger van that had pulled up out front. "Looks like the Cedarwood Long Term Care community is here for Bingo night," he said. "I read it in the calendar announcements that were posted in the activity room. Tell me, though, what are you trying to say?"

"Violet and I got together," Kiko said.

"And?"

"It's not all about *you*," Kiko said. "Violet said she has absolutely no feelings for you, but she was annoyed with me because we're breaking the rules, and in this case, the rules are there for good reason. Plus, she admitted that I just annoy her in general, though she owned up to the fact that that's ridiculousness." She paused and let out a long breath. "We should've told Claire about Sanchez, about the lipstick thing, immediately. And I think I didn't do the right thing because of *us*. We both need to make decisions based on what is right, not based on protecting a boyfriend or girlfriend."

Jack turned around from the front seat to face her. "I was starting to think of us that way as well. But you're right. I thought I'd get a little more proof that Sanchez was the guy, or at least one of the guys, then shove it in Fitz's face. I was probably trying to impress you."

Kiko closed her eyes, a pained expression spreading across her face. "I know," she said, "and I let you do it. What if Sanchez had been let go and it turned out he *was* the guy." She shook her head. "That's why we have to end it."

Jack glanced back at the entrance, where a steady stream

of people were exiting the small passenger van, some walking quickly, some hobbling with canes.

"I do understand," Jack said. "If I were in your position, I'd choose this task force over dating me as well."

"Don't think of it like that," Kiko said. "I don't want to put Claire in the position where she has to tell us to break it off. She'd hate herself for doing that, but she'd be right to do it. So *we* have to do it. Plus, and this is a whole other thing, you and I are like firecrackers, Jack. We're pyrotechnic works of art. But what happens when our fuses are tied too close together? *BOOM!* You and I both know this ends in smoke and ashes." She sighed, then put on an exaggerated British accent, like she'd just fallen from a Jane Austen novel into the back of the SUV to deliver one final message. "My darling Mr. Russo, I find animals quite insufferable and you absolutely abhor ice cream. We're from two different worlds. Our union would be a terrible blunder."

Jack chuckled, then went quiet, listening to the rain on the roof of the SUV. It came down in an odd pattern, pouring down in short bursts, then easing into something closer to a mist.

"I get it," he said.

He turned again to face her and she had what he read as a hopeful look on her face, a look that asked, *Can we still be friends?* Or maybe it said, *I hope we work effectively together as colleagues despite the obvious attraction between us.*

"I really was getting pretty serious about you, though," Jack said. "I even thought I might take you out for ice cream."

CHAPTER FORTY-TWO

I'VE BEEN WAITING in the parking lot for hours, biding my time, looking for my opportunity.

Earlier, as the sun set, casting an orange glow over the parking lot, I considered pretending to be a family member. That wouldn't have worked. I didn't know the name of any other resident at the facility.

But I see my opportunity now.

The lettering on the white van reads Cedarwood Long Term Care. I see the many heads of gray hair through the windows as it pulls in front of the building. The only other occupied car in the lot is no threat.

The bald and handsome man sitting in the front could definitely be a cop, but he isn't paying attention. He is turned around looking into the back seat, and it looks like he's speaking with someone.

The van holds at least eighteen people, and I pull my shawl tight around my hair and hurry to cross the parking lot blending in with them as they enter.

I follow the group toward the sitting area, reading each name on the door as I pass.

There it is.

I see his door off to the right, but a police officer is sitting out front.

I veer toward the restroom and once inside, stare at myself in the mirror.

I wonder if I look like she would have. Would lines have put grooves around her mouth and would her chubby froggy face have eventually sunken too?

All those years ago I had no choice. I had to let those women be hurt, every one of them was my mother. The woman I hurt recently was my mother, too.

I take a few deep breaths to prepare myself and then leave the bathroom, ready to harm as many as necessary to reach the person I need to hurt most of all.

I smile at the guard as I walk past. He looks young and naive. The type who would run through a house on fire to save a kid—and do so again if the kid left his kitten.

When I'm sure the guard isn't looking, I duck into a room with an open door.

The woman in the room doesn't stir. There is a machine next to her bed that, with all of its blinking lights and bags dripping mysterious fluids, looks important. I take my chances that it is and bite through the tubing that runs from the machine into the woman's arm until I taste salty and bitter fluid and stroll out again.

I head back toward the bingo game, which is just about to begin.

I can hear the beeping coming from the woman's room and two nurses rush by.

The security guard doesn't move. He must not know what the beeping means.

I know I am acting strange and someone will notice soon. I have to make a quick decision.

Sitting down at one of the bingo tables, I put my purse

in my lap and with my hands under the table, I pull out the steak knife I took from the diner. The woman to my left has a little name tag that says *Sister Ella*. It is ironic, a bunch of old women in a Memory Care Facility playing bingo. Half of them probably can't remember their names. How are they supposed to place markers on their cards if they can't remember what they've just heard?

With a quick jolt, I thrust the knife toward her leg, busting through her thin pants and impaling her calf.

She falls back, screaming in pain.

I stand up. "Oh my God, what happened?" I yell.

I jog down the hall toward the security guard, pointing back at the table. "A woman just stabbed the other woman. Get her!"

The security guard stands and glances back at his door, then at the scene unfolding before him. I see him make up his mind in a flash and he races toward Sister Ella.

I open the door to Augustus's room, walk in, and close it behind me.

"You haven't forgotten me, have you?" I say, smiling. "You haven't forgotten your little cousin Cecelia, your precious little lover, Taylor."

CHAPTER FORTY-THREE

"WHAT IS IT?" Claire asked Thacker. "What do you know?"

He looked down at her and a smile spread over his face. Then he leaned in and tried to kiss her.

"No," Claire said, pushing him away. "What the hell are you thinking?"

"Oh, come on," he laughed. "You're literally stalking me."

"I... what?" Claire let out an exasperated sigh. "So you don't know anything? This was all..."

He leaned in again and she pushed him away, more forcefully this time. "Do I need to remind you that I'm armed?"

Fitz was right about this jerk all along. She was about to tell him off when she heard something—muffled shouts, possibly. Or wait, what was that? She followed the sound around the back of the building where she saw agents Mary and Hector.

"What is it?" Claire shouted.

"Someone just drew the blinds in the room you asked us to watch. It didn't look like a nurse."

Claire leapt over the curb, through a couple of bushes, and hurried to the window of Cunningham's room. Standing on her tiptoes, she tried to peek in, but the blinds covered every inch of the window. Pressing her ear against it, she listened, but heard nothing.

Then there *was* a sound—a wicked sound. A screech like a dying cat or a car in desperate need of new brake pads. She raced over to the back door of the facility, which was locked. Shooting looks around the parking lot, she didn't see Thacker. Most likely, he'd gone back inside when he'd been rebuffed.

Taking off at full speed around the side of the building, she made it to the front entrance and didn't ask for permission. Bolting through the front door, she raced down the hallway past a commotion and an old woman being led away on a stretcher, bleeding from her leg. Claire thought it might be Sister Ella.

She reached Cunningham's door. A young police officer was there.

"What the hell happened?" Claire asked.

"A lady got stabbed during the bingo game. I don't know. It all happened so fast." He held up both hands as though this would shield him from any culpability in the matter. "There was a woman... she—"

"Describe the woman," Claire barked.

"Seventy years old, maybe. Gray hair, a shawl over her head. She looked, I don't know, like an old lady but spry and... oh, I don't know."

Claire tried the handle, but it was locked. She knew that this sort of door had safety locks. It could be locked from the inside, but a master key controlled every single door in the facility. She turned and looked around, seeing Thacker at the end of the hallway. She hurried up to him.

"There's a killer in with Cunningham. Open the door now."

~

"Wait," Jack said suddenly, squinting into the dimly lit parking lot. "Where is Claire? I mean, why isn't she back yet?"

He glanced at the front entrance. Everything was quiet, but still, something didn't feel right.

"I'm going in," he said, and with that, he swung open the door and hurried across the parking lot, dodging puddles. He heard a door slam behind him and knew that Kiko was right on his trail.

The woman at the entry desk tried to stop him, but he rushed past her down the hall where he saw Claire and a young officer. Thacker was there as well, fumbling with some keys.

"Claire," Jack called.

She looked over, and her eyes told him everything he needed to know. The door was locked, and someone, probably Cecelia Fontenot, was in the room with Cunningham.

"Damn!" Jack put a hand on Kiko's shoulder. "We are going around back."

They bolted down the hall and out the side door, then curled around the corner of the building. The two young agents were still posted out back, seemingly oblivious to what was going on.

At the window to Cunningham's room, Jack examined the frame. He wedged his fingers under to see if he could pop it out, but it wasn't even close. This was solid, old-school construction.

Kiko was right next to him. "I might be able to climb up the brick outcroppings and swing in to kick through the window."

"That's too dangerous," Jack said. "Even for me."

Kiko gave him a look but said nothing.

"I have an idea," Jack said. He pulled his cell phone out of his back pocket and dialed Fitz.

When Fitz answered, Jack said, "Cecelia Fontenot has locked herself in the room with Gus. Is there anything you can say to get her not to kill him?"

As he spoke, he was rushing through the back door and up the hallway to the information desk.

Fitz replied, "I'll try."

CHAPTER FORTY-FOUR

I PULL the belt out of my purse and uncoil it slowly.

It's the only memento I kept, and maybe I did so because I always knew it would come to this.

Gus was always interested in photographs, but the belt, for me, is the thing. It symbolizes the moment of my freedom and the moment of my imprisonment in a new kind of cell.

Now it will set me free again.

I ignore the banging on the wall, the banging on the door, and the window. I have slid the thick wooden wedge under the door so they can't bust through, even if they have the key. And now all my attention is on Gus, who appears to be hanging on by a thread.

"Do you remember?" I ask.

He's lying in his bed, blinking. Does he even recognize me?

I lean in closer. "Do you remember?"

"I forget nothing," he says, and his voice is weak, far away. "We forget nothing. I became the crane."

I hold up the belt in front of his weakly blinking eyes.

The last time I saw him, he still had a full head of hair. Now his scalp is bald and pasty gray, like he hasn't seen the sun in five years, maybe longer.

I hear shouting outside the door and the rattling of keys.

"You lied to me," I say. "I was never adopted."

He opens his mouth to speak, then closes it. His eyes widen, and for a moment, I think he is dead.

"You lied, and now you're going to die," I say. "You know what the rules are. No one hurts your Taylor. Now I am the crane."

His eyes open suddenly. "I needed to have you. I saved you and you were mine. And when I had you, it was something I was meant to do. Women should not hurt their little nephews. And they should not hurt their little children."

I make a loop with the belt and place it around his neck. "But uncles should not lie to their little nieces."

With all of the women, Gus was the one who did the strangling.

I studied how he did it, though, and I never forgot.

I remembered, and I remember now.

CHAPTER FORTY-FIVE

"I NEED access to the facility-wide PA system immediately," Jack said, skidding to a stop in front of the information desk.

The man there held up a hand to object, but Jack made his eyes as hard as he could and held up his badge.

"I'm not supposed to do this," he grumbled. "You people aren't even supposed to be here." But while he spoke he handed Jack a little black device that looked like half of a walkie-talkie connected to a cord.

Jack grabbed it and leaned across the desk. "Okay, Fitz. Tell me what to say."

"If I'd known I was going to play Cyrano de Bergerac today, I would have prepared."

"No time for jokes, Fitz. Go."

"I was thinking while I was joking. Here's what to say..."

～

Claire could hear the muffled sounds of quiet speech from Cunningham's the room. The police officer still stood next to her, dumbfounded. Thacker finally got the right key in the lock and it clicked open. Claire pushed on the door but it caught immediately.

"These are extra heavy fire doors," Thacker said. "She's got it blocked."

Claire reared back and lowered her shoulder, springing forward with all her aggression.

The door didn't budge.

"I'm telling you," Thacker said, "a patient did this once and it took the fire department to get him out. They've already been called."

Claire heard sirens in the distance and pounded on the door, but she knew it was futile. Then she heard a voice emerge from the little black speakers in the corners of the hallway. It was the facility's sound system.

"Cecelia, don't do this. He always loved you and he never lied."

It was Jack's voice.

"Cecelia, you may have seen me on the television. I was the young guy. The handsome one. The brilliant psychologist. I lied about you not being adopted. We were trying to get you to come here, to seek vengeance, but it was all a lie. Don't kill him. You *are* adopted. It's true. You were never related. Augustus Cunningham told you the truth because he loved you. He probably still loves you. Even after everything you two have done, he still loves you."

The sirens were right outside the building now and Claire was still pushing on the door with everything she had.

"And there's a reason to let him live," Jack continued. "He doesn't know about Michael, about your son. He deserves to meet his son before he dies."

∽

I listen to the man on the intercom and watch Gus's eyes fill with tears at the mention of Michael.

"Is this true?" I ask. "Is it true that they lied? I really am adopted?"

Gus looks at me, blinking away the tears. "I don't know," he says. "I can't remember. I know... I know *some* things. I know I always wished we weren't related so we could... But it was so long ago... I... I forget."

He tries to sit up, but he's too weak. He closes his eyes. "Do I have a son? Do I have a son?"

"You do," I say. "I got pregnant, and that's why I left. After Yreka. I didn't want him to be near any part of what we'd become. Any part of what you turned me into. I wanted him to have a chance to be normal."

"Is he normal?" Gus asks, closing his eyes.

Someone is smashing at the door now and it creaks and groans violently.

"He is."

Gus opens his eyes suddenly. "I remember now. I made it up. We *are* cousins. I did it because I saved you and you were mine. I had to have you."

He looks at me, eyes imploring. I know he's telling the truth, and I tighten the belt around his neck, squeezing with all I have until he goes limp.

So limp that he can't see me nodding. "He's normal," I say, just as I hear the sound of shattering glass. "And he's the only good thing in this rotten hell of a world."

Claire stood to the side as the pair of firemen swung their metal battering ram, the thick wood splintering with each thrust. The door, wedged shut from the inside, groaned and creaked. Sweat dripped off them as they put their full weight into another strike. Finally, with a resounding crack, the door gave way, and they burst through.

Claire was right behind them, stepping into the room just as she heard the sound of shattering glass. She looked up to see Kiko swinging into the room through the broken window, leading the way with her boots.

Cecelia Fontenot was hovering over the bed, holding a belt that had been pulled tight around Augustus Cunningham's neck.

"The only good thing," she was whispering. "The only good thing."

Claire hurried forward and grabbed Cecelia by the shoulders. She was poised for a confrontation, but Cecelia didn't resist.

"He's gone," she whispered. "Soon I'll be gone. But Michael will remain. He's not like us. He's good. And there's nothing he needs to forget."

CHAPTER FORTY-SIX

HALF AN HOUR LATER, Claire sat on the bumper of the SUV, watching Kiko get treated for a series of cuts around her ankles and calves.

"Did you okay that?" she asked Jack, who had come up and joined her.

"I told her it was too dangerous for me to attempt," he said, "which I thought was like telling her not to do it."

Claire laughed. "With Kiko, she's going to take that as a challenge." She paused, letting her head fall back to take in the starless night sky. "What were you doing inside the facility?"

"Checking on Sister Ella. The wound was only half an inch deep. She got some stitches and is going to be okay. Oddly, the attack seems to have made her *more* lucid. We spoke in Italian for over five minutes." He smiled. "That lady has some stories, and I'm going to come back and check on her tomorrow. I also found Michael Butterman, Cecelia's son," he said. "Do you want to talk to him?" Jack held up his phone, where a phone number had been dialed into a FaceTime call. "Just press send."

She took the phone from Jack, lowering her head when she heard the sound of a vehicle pulling through the parking lot. It was the ambulance into which Cecelia Fontenot had been placed a few minutes earlier. She was on her way to a high-security psychiatric prison. She had killed Augustus Cunningham with the same belt he'd used to kill her mother and five other women. The same one she'd used to kill the woman in Portland. Now the belt was in an evidence bag, and Cecelia Fontenot would spend the rest of her life, however short that was, in a psychiatric prison.

Claire pressed send and held the phone in front of her face, aligning it so that it didn't show anything identifiable as an ambulance in the background. A man appeared on her screen, maybe thirty-five years old, Caucasian with brown hair and glasses.

"Hello," he said. "Who is this?"

"Claire Anderson, special agent with the Seattle FBI. I have some difficult news."

He swallowed hard and stifled what appeared to be a grimace. "Tell me a little bit about yourself, please. How do I know you are actually with the FBI?"

She held her badge up in front of the phone. "I'm here in Seattle. Your mother has just been arrested. Cecelia Fontenot is your mother, correct?"

He nodded. "Cecelia Butterman, but yeah. I knew she'd changed her name, and I haven't seen her in fifteen years."

"Well, she's alive and on her way to prison."

Claire watched the look on his face, trying to figure out whether Michael, the product of this incestuous relationship, was "normal," as Cecelia had said.

He seemed to be thinking long and hard, and then finally he spoke. "I don't want to know," he said. "I don't want to know what she did, why she was arrested." He grimaced as though reliving some old pain. "When I was sixteen or seventeen, I started to know that my mother was a dark, dark person. She was fighting demons. Maybe she wasn't pure evil, but she told me once that she had seen evil and she'd never forget it. I got into the University of California at Santa Cruz when I was only seventeen years old. I went and I never looked back. The truth is, I want to remember her as someone who tried her best. Someone who escaped whatever evil she escaped. I don't want to know what she did." He paused, closing his eyes. "I don't ever want to know."

Michael Butterman ended the call, and Claire handed the phone back to Jack.

"He's going to have to find out at some point," Jack said.

Claire nodded. "I don't know why, but it makes me feel a little bit better to think that he might really have escaped. That he never knew his father, Augustus Cunningham. And that he knew something was off about his mother and was able to escape without committing murder. We're going to have to look into him, but for now, I'm going to take peace in the fact that it appears as though he is a moral person, leading a normal life."

Jack nodded.

"I was listening to a song the other day on my drive into the office," Claire continued. "Folk song by I don't know who... there was a phrase in it, 'The hell inside us.' It stuck with me. Something about Michael..." She felt tears rising in her eyes and wiped them away quickly, embarrassed.

"What is it?" Jack asked.

"If anyone had the hell inside them, it was his parents. I just hope he can be free."

After a long silence, Jack said, "You know, that was Fitz telling me what to say over the intercom. We were trying to stall. To give you long enough to get in."

Claire looked at the ground watching a pigeon amble

around puddles and nibble on the occasional piece of soggy popcorn. Even with this case closed, she had a mess on her hands. It felt as though her task force was fraying at the edges—one loose thread tugged at just the right angle could destroy it.

"There's something else I want to tell you," Jack said. He nodded at Kiko, who was walking over to them, limping slightly. "Kiko and I have been having a relationship. You already knew that. But I wanted you to hear it from me, and I want you to know now that it's over."

Claire looked at Jack, then at Kiko. "Jack is telling me it's over, Kiko. Is that true?"

Kiko nodded.

Claire let out a sigh. "I didn't want to have to be the one to end it, and I didn't want to have to transfer either of you."

"I appreciate that," Kiko said. "And I'm sorry for putting you in that position. We good?"

She believed they were telling the truth, at least as they understood it. But when it came to love, sometimes people were less in charge than they thought they were.

Claire stood up and gave Kiko a brief hug.

Jack stood and extended a hand, which she shook.

"We're good," she said to both of them.

She hoped it was true.

CHAPTER FORTY-SEVEN

THE NEXT DAY, Claire had the meeting she'd been dreading.

Hightower had called the meeting for first thing in the morning, so at 7:55, Claire paced the hallway near Kathy's desk, trying not to make eye contact with her as she sipped her cappuccino. Kathy had always been a friend, and she knew she supported S.W.O.R.D., but she didn't want to put her in an awkward position. If she was going to catch hell from Hightower, she didn't want Kathy to feel awkward setting up the meeting at which she had to do so.

Cecelia Fontenot had been secured in a psychiatric prison, charged with multiple murders, including that of her cousin and lover, and the father of her child, Augustus Cunningham. The night before, Claire had leaked much of what had happened to the local press. The public was clamoring for information, and she wanted this thing to be settled as soon as possible.

Early that morning, the story was on the front page of most of the newspapers in the country and was leading the major news networks on television. Claire declined multiple requests for interviews, as she always did. Other than the paperwork, she was ready to put the case of the Interstate Reaper behind her.

She heard Hightower's door creak open and was surprised to see the face of Jonathan Rivera, expressionless as ever. He wore a tan suit and a crisp white shirt and glared at her as he stopped at Kathy's desk.

Glancing down, he said, "It's been nice knowing you, Kathy," and reached out to shake her hand.

Then he walked straight up to Claire and stood looking into her eyes, his wide, stout frame blocking her path to Hightower's office. He opened his mouth to speak, but thought better of it, shook his head, and walked away down the hallway to the elevators.

Hightower stood at the doorway and invited her in.

"What was that about?" she asked as she sat down.

"He's being transferred."

Claire felt a grin spread across her face. "Transferred out of this office, you mean?"

"Quantico, Virginia. He did such a good job cutting costs here they're sending him to the Mothership."

Claire thought of a few friends and colleagues she had at the main FBI office in Quantico. Her smile faded. Then, just as quickly, it returned. "They are going to absolutely hate him. I need to call some people to warn them."

"He asked me to let you go because of that whole helicopter stunt."

Claire's face grew stern. "One of my team had been attacked, and we'd gotten the evidence we needed in Portland. There was no way we were going to take three hours to drive back."

"Okay, okay." Hightower held up both hands. "I'm not a witness, and you're not a prosecutor. The expense is fine, and you have a second car now. Rivera's Escalade. Not to mention, check your office downstairs. I got you a cappuccino machine on my own dime. Top of the line. I didn't know there was such a thing as an $800 home cappuccino machine, but Kathy said it was one of the best."

"You can easily spend twice that much," Claire said.

Hightower frowned.

"I mean, thank you." Claire stood. "And you're welcome to come down for coffee anytime you like."

"I like my coffee weak, black, and lukewarm," Hightower said, reaching across the table to shake her hand. "Before you go though, Claire, two more things."

Claire sat back down, and Hightower did as well.

"Sanchez," Hightower said.

"He's clear in this thing, still being held for the assault on Jack though."

"If it's alright with you, we're gonna cut him a deal. He's got a lot of inside scoops from his time in prison. Might be able to give us a murder or two."

Claire waved it away. "Fine, fine." She didn't love the idea of a guy like Sanchez walking free, but deals like this got made every day. "What's the second thing?"

"Fitz," Hightower said. "Am I right that he got drunk in the Boiler Room the other night and slept on the floor?"

Claire couldn't lie to him, but she wasn't going to give Fitz up either.

She sat stone-faced, saying nothing.

"I got a report from the cleaning crew. He scared them half to death." Hightower let out a long breath. "I think you know, Claire, that I'm not above hearing from people further down in the hierarchy, but do you really think it's a good use of my time to be fielding reports about a drunken giant from the *cleaning crew*?"

Claire grimaced. "I'm sorry. I'll handle it."

"I know you need to protect your guy, and I respect it. I

would do the same. But Claire, he's a loose cannon. And not like Jack or Kiko busting through that window. And believe me, we are going to talk about that as well. He's a more dangerous sort of loose cannon. Psychologically wild, influenceable, and unpredictable."

"I know," Claire said. "I really know that. But we need him."

Hightower held up a piece of paper. "I *know* you need him. That's what I'm talking about. He put in for a transfer. Cited personal reasons. Said he no longer wants to be a part of S.W.O.R.D." He raised an eyebrow. "And I know how much he needs this job, and how much he admires you. So I guess what I'm saying is..." He trailed off.

Claire looked at the paper. She recognized Fitz's sloppy handwriting. It didn't mention her, but Claire knew immediately why he'd requested the transfer. And it seemed as though Hightower might know as well.

"Technically," Hightower said, "he's a consultant and doesn't even need to request a transfer. Of course, he never bothered to read the paperwork that explains that. No one else has to take him on, but people will. The counterterrorism team needs a psych guy. Hell, everyone could use Fitz if they knew how to corral him."

"It's a tough job," Claire said. "One that's taken me years to perfect. And I may not be as good at it as I thought."

"Well," Hightower said, standing and handing Claire the paper, "you better try to get him back in the fold. Because I can't make him stay."

∾

Claire had moved her chair away from the table and was now throwing a tennis ball gently against the wall so that it would bounce one time before Ranger, who was sitting at her feet, would leap up and catch it out of the air.

"Seven," she said. "Seven in a row."

Violet, who was sitting at the computers, said, "Eleven is the record. At least that's what Jack claims to have gotten."

Claire tossed the ball again. It struck the wall, bounced on the carpet, and up in the air like it would fall right into her lap. Ranger stood on his hind legs, nabbed it, then handed it back to her politely.

"He may not be able to smell much," she said, "but his dexterity is still there, especially for such an old dog."

"I wanted to say, Violet," Claire said, "I appreciate the way you handled things with Jack and Kiko."

"Don't mention it," Violet said without looking over.

Claire stood and walked over to her, placing a hand on her shoulder. "Really, in my day, this might have turned into a whole messy love triangle piece of nonsense. The way you young ladies handled it was impressive. I know I wouldn't have handled it as well at your age." She thought for a moment, considering her brief, disastrous flirtation with Thacker. "Not sure I'd handle it as well *now*."

Violet turned, her lips slightly curled downward. "It helps that Jack is a meathead." She said it with a hint of derision, but Claire thought it was feigned. Or perhaps that she was trying to convince herself of something. "The three of us are getting dinner tonight. To celebrate the end of the case and forge a new path forward."

Claire smiled down at Violet. "Glad to hear it." She needed the three of them to be on good terms, especially if she was going to lose Fitz.

Claire returned to the ball game, but was interrupted after two more throws when Fitz came in, whistling the *waltzing through purgatory* song he'd been singing a couple of nights earlier.

"Can I speak with you?" Claire asked, nodding toward the hall.

Fitz pulled a large rawhide bone out of a paper bag and handed it to an excited Ranger, who looked up at him gratefully, then bolted to the corner where he curled up with it.

Claire led Fitz into the hallway and closed the door behind them. Glancing up and down to make sure they were alone, she said, "We need to talk."

"That's what I came here to do," Fitz said.

She leaned against the wall. "Then you go first."

He stood up straight and ran his meaty hands over his wrinkled brown jacket. Apparently he'd given up on the new blue one. "One of the great messages in *The Inferno* is that there can be no progress, no personal growth, no ascension to heaven, without first admitting to one's own sin."

"Fitz, for once, can you just talk like a person? No psychological BS. No literary references."

He ignored her. "I myself, as you know, do not believe in sin, at least not in the religious sense. There's no one up there judging us, there's no right and wrong, only the law of the animals and whatever moral codes we can force ourselves to believe in for our short time on earth. I don't believe in sin, but I know I am a deeply imperfect person." He looked away, and Claire saw a quiver in his chin. "I know I'm not someone you could ever love. That's why I can't work with you anymore." He looked at her and his eyes betrayed a hope that his words hadn't. "I know Violet spoke with you," he continued. "It's embarrassing, but it is what it is. Life is ultimately one long, embarrassing waltz through purgatory anyway. The great mess, the great chaos you've always feared is here, and it's taken the form of a three-hundred pound British drunk who loves you."

"You *don't* love me, Fitz."

"I do."

"You don't. And you *can* work with me. Once you realize you don't love me, everything will work out."

"Do you remember the first time we worked together?" he asked, looking directly at her, his eyes slightly moist.

She nodded. "It was your first case consulting with the FBI in Seattle. The triple homicide."

He smiled. "That's right. We'd worked together for about a week on that, and the day we finally arrested our perp, do you remember what you said to me?"

Claire thought back, but she honestly couldn't remember. The case had been one of the most gruesome she'd ever seen, and, by the end, she'd been running on fumes.

"I know what you're thinking," Fitz said. "You don't remember what you said, you were exhausted, it didn't mean anything, and *blah blah blah*." He paused, holding his face stiff to fight back the tears. "You told me the UK was missing out, and that my father would be proud of me." He paused. "And that's the thing about you, Claire. Even when you are on automatic, at your worst, you're *still* a good person. You make me believe that sin might be real, and that some people are above it."

Claire shook her head. "I'm definitely not above it."

"No," he said. "You think I'm idealizing you the way Dante did with Beatrice, but I'm not. I see you, Claire. I *know* you. I think you know that I know you. I see your flaws, too, and you're still perfect. That's why I put in for a transfer. I know you can't love me. And I know I can't work with you anymore."

"Fitz, I—"

He held up a hand. "I know you won't ever love me, Claire, but I can't stand having to face that fact every single day."

CHAPTER FORTY-EIGHT

"BENNY," Claire said, "you know that you bring me so much happiness."

Benny set down the controller and looked over. They were sitting cross-legged on the floor in front of the television. Having defeated her fifteen straight times in a one-versus-one match in *Fish Wars 2*, he smiled. "Is that why you let me win?" he asked.

"I do not."

"I know you don't. But, you are getting a little bit better. I actually had to dodge one time during our last match."

Claire scoffed playfully. "Actually, I've been thinking about starting my own YouTube channel. It's going to be called 'FBI Agent Mom Who Is Totally Cracked at *Fish Wars* and Is a Gamer Baller Bro.' Does that sound like a good name?"

Benny groaned. "Mom, stop."

"But, *bro*," she continued, trying to sound like a thirteen-year-old gamer, "I'm going to go off in *Fish Wars II*, because I am the Ultimate Rizzler."

"Where did you even hear half of these terms?" Benny asked, flushing red with embarrassment.

"Oh, I think you know where I heard them," Claire said. "From *you*. Don't think I don't watch your videos just because you don't see me do it. Sometimes at work I take a ten-minute coffee break and watch your latest. What is a *Rizzler*, anyway?"

"Someone who has *rizz*, obviously."

Claire raised an eyebrow.

"Rizz is like charisma, Mom. And you do *not* have it. You have many fine qualities, but rizz is not one of them."

Claire stood up and turned off the TV. "Whatever happened with that gaming company?"

"I talked with Dad about it, and he convinced me it wasn't a good idea. Said they might be taking advantage of me. Using my channel to promote their games without fair compensation."

Claire had been concerned about the partnership as well, but she hadn't wanted to burst his balloon. But Benny actually sounded pretty positive about it.

"Dad said," he continued, "that I'd have thousands of opportunities in the coming years and that I should hold out for my true worth." His voice cracked as he spoke, and Claire felt tears welling in her eyes. "Plus," he continued, "he's taking me fishing next weekend. Got us rods and everything."

Benny and her ex-husband hadn't had many great moments together, and hearing this thawed a part of her that had been long frozen. Benny was at the age, though, where he didn't love showing sadness or emotion in front of his mom.

He hopped up and hurried to the kitchen to pour himself a glass of juice.

Later, Claire sat out on her deck, taking in the light of the golden hour and sipping a glass of local cabernet.

Her phone rang. It was Sy.

"That was some case you just put to bed. You doing okay?" Sy asked.

Claire stood and walked to the edge of the deck. "You heard?"

"Who *didn't* hear about it?" Sy replied. "It was front-page news everywhere."

"Yeah, I guess it would be."

"I was surprised you didn't mention dating your colleague on the phone the other night," Sy said.

"What?"

"You and Fitz..."

"Double what?"

"Thacker, the Executive Director guy, was quoted saying your team had been deeply unprofessional and that you were having an inappropriate relationship with a British psych profiler on your team named Fitzgerald Pembroke. I need to get the tea."

"The tea?"

"It's what young people say," Sy said. "It means gossip."

Claire returned to the little wooden table and watched golden light dance off the water. "I guess it's no surprise that he's trying to make me look bad in the papers. After a brief flirtation, I felt some red flags and turned him down."

"What an utter slimeball," Sy said. "So, there's nothing between you and this Fitz guy?"

"No." Claire didn't want to talk about it.

Hightower told her that he hadn't been assigned to a new unit yet, but she hadn't heard from Fitz since their meeting in the hallway outside the Boiler Room. She had no idea when she'd hear from him again, if ever. For now, Violet, Kiko, and Jack were still part of the team. Things were settled. Or, at least, settled enough to move forward.

"There's... there's something else," Sy said. "The real reason I called."

She sounded upset. "What's wrong?" Claire asked. "Don't tell me Austin turned out to be a bastard, too."

"No, no signs of that yet, thank goodness." Sy laughed. "No, it's just... I've been thinking about your case since we last spoke, Flaggler, the cult, Moses Lake. I really hope you don't mind, but I brought it up casually at this law enforcement wine club in New Haven that I've been going to. Long story short, I ended up chatting with someone who was on the inter-agency task force."

In addition to local law-enforcement, there had been a joint FBI-ATF-Homeland Security Task Force investigation. They had concluded that the story was as simple as it was horrific. Charismatic cult leader Thomson Flaggler had convinced three-dozen of his followers that divine intervention would soon freeze time, leaving everyone on earth stuck in a state of eternal punishment for the sins of humanity. To escape this fate and guarantee an endless communion with the divine, followers drank diluted wine mixed with valium and cyanide. Everyone on the commune died. Everyone except Claire.

"He hinted," Sy continued, "that there was a lot more to the story—things that never made it into the press and, more importantly, things that never made it into the official report."

The deck seemed to tilt suddenly, Claire's reality skewing at the edges.

"He said that he'd be happy to talk about it off the record, if you ever wanted."

For a split second, Claire felt as though she was sliding

down the embankment onto the beach below. She came to —safely sitting on the deck—and to her relief, still cradling her glass of wine.

She blinked rapidly, heart racing, but she made her voice as steady as she could. "That's a lot to take in," she said. Sy speaking with a handful of people about her actual past and Thacker live-streaming defamatory lies about her were two wildly different scenarios, but both left her feeling exposed. And fragile. "I'm sure I'll want to talk with him. Give me a few weeks?"

"Of course," Sy said. "Take all the time you need."

"Thanks for thinking of me," Claire said. She realized it would take some getting used to but that's what girlfriends do, they think of each other. She took a long sip of her cabernet. "Oh yeah, I need to share something important with you as well."

"What's that?" Sy asked.

"It's this Washington State cabernet. Let's not talk about my past anymore, and let's not talk about men." Claire smiled to herself. "Let's talk about wine."

—The End—

Thanks for reading! If you're enjoying this series, check out Book 3, *Widows of Medina*, which comes out in the fall of 2024.

A NOTE FROM THE AUTHOR

Thanks for reading!

If you enjoyed this book, I encourage you to check out the whole series of FBI Task Force S.W.O.R.D. novels. Each book can be read as a standalone, although relationships and situations develop from book to book, so they will be more enjoyable if read in order.

And if you're loving S.W.O.R.D., check out my first hit series of fast-paced Pacific Northwest mysteries: the Thomas Austin Crime Thrillers.

I also have an online store, where you can buy signed paperbacks, mugs, t-shirts, and more featuring the S.W.O.R.D. team's lovable golden retriever, Ranger, as well as locations and quotations from all my books. Check that out on my website.

Every day I feel fortunate to be able to wake up and create characters and write stories. And that's all made possible by readers like you. So, again, I extend my heartfelt thanks for checking out my books, and I wish you hundreds of hours of happy reading to come.

D.D. Black

MORE D.D. BLACK NOVELS

ABOUT D.D. BLACK

D.D. Black is the author of the Thomas Austin Crime Thrillers, the FBI Task Force S.W.O.R.D. series, and other Pacific Northwest crime novels. When he's not writing, he can be found strolling the beaches of the Pacific Northwest, cooking dinner for his wife and kids, or throwing a ball for his corgi over and over and over. Find out more at ddblack author.com.

facebook.com/ddblackauthor

instagram.com/ddblackauthor

tiktok.com/@d.d.black

amazon.com/D-D-Black/e/B0B6H2XTTP

bookbub.com/profile/d-d-black

Made in the USA
Columbia, SC
26 June 2024